ROBOT WARS

SIGMUND BROUWER

BOOK FOUR

COUNTER-ATTACK

TYNDALE HOUSE PUBLISHERS, INC.
CAROL STREAM, ILLINOIS

You can contact Sigmund Brouwer through his website at www.coolreading.com or www.whomadethemoon.com.

Visit Tyndale's exciting website for kids at www.tyndale.com/kids.

TYNDALE and Tyndale's quill logo are registered trademarks of Tyndale House Publishers, Inc.

Counterattack

Previously published as Mars Diaries *Mission 7: Countdown* and Mars Diaries *Mission 8: Robot War* under ISBNs 0-8423-4310-5 and 0-8423-4311-3.

Counterattack first published in 2009.

Designed by Mark Anthony Lane II

For manufacturing information regarding this product, please call 1-800-323-9400.

Library of Congress Cataloging-in-Publication Data

Brouwer, Sigmund, date.
  Counterattack / Sigmund Brouwer.
    p. cm. — (Robot wars ; bk. 4)
  Previously published separately in 2001 as Mars Diaries, Mission 7: Countdown; and Mars Diaries, Mission 8: Robot War.
  Summary: In the first of two adventures set in 2040, fourteen-year-old, wheelchair-bound, virtual reality specialist, Tyce Sanders, finds himself in grave danger on his first trip to Earth, and in the second, Tyce must use all his skills to find a way to stop the slaughter of the governors of the World United Federation.
  ISBN 978-1-4143-2312-1 (softcover)
  [1. Science fiction. 2. Robots—Fiction. 3. People with disabilities—Fiction. 4. Virtual reality—Fiction. 5. Christian life—Fiction.] I. Brouwer, Sigmund, date. Mars diaries. Mission 7, Countdown. II. Brouwer, Sigmund, date. Mars diaries. Mission 8, Robot war. III. Title.

PZ7.B79984Cou 2009
[Fic]—dc22   2009016771

Printed in the United States of America

17 16 15 14 13 12 11
 8   7   6   5   4   3   2

THIS SERIES IS DEDICATED
IN MEMORY OF MARTYN GODFREY.

*Martyn, you wrote books that reached all of
us kids at heart. You wrote them because you
really cared. We all miss you.*

FROM THE AUTHOR

We live in amazing times! When I first began writing these
Mars journals, not even 40 years after our technology allowed
us to put men on the moon, the concept of robot control was
strictly something I daydreamed about when readers first
met Tyce. Since then, science fiction has been science fact.
Successful experiments have now been performed on monkeys
who are able to use their brains to control robots halfway
around the world!

Suddenly it's not so far-fetched to believe that these
adventures could happen for Tyce. Or for you. Or for your
children.

With that in mind, I hope you enjoy stepping into a
future that could really happen. . . .

Sigmund Brouwer

JOURNAL
ONE

CHAPTER 1

Neuron rifles.

Twenty soldiers—in full protective gear, including black uniforms, black helmets, dark mirrored visors—each held a rifle aimed directly at my head. The voltage of just one neuron rifle would cripple me with the pain of an electrical jolt through the nerve pathways of my body.

But 20 neuron rifles fired at me all at once? With the nerve pathways too scrambled to give instructions to my muscles, I wouldn't even be able to scream as I died.

Each of those soldiers followed my slow progress by keeping me in the sights of their weapons. I had nowhere to run. Nowhere to hide.

Only moments earlier, the robot that carried me in its arms had arrived to take me out of my prison cell. I'd grabbed my comp-board—my fold-up laptop computer—in the few seconds I had to gather my belongings. I had left behind my wheelchair from Mars, since it was useless. The prison officials had removed its wheels on the remote chance I'd find a way to escape. Now as the robot wheeled down the wide, white corridor of this military prison, the soldiers surrounded me, front and back.

Carried as I was by the robot, I felt like a baby. Worse, if the robot set me down, the best I'd be able to do was crawl by using my arms to pull me forward. I was without my wheel-chair, and after a lifetime on Mars, I struggled with the extra gravity on Earth.

The squeak of the robot's wheels provided a steady back-drop to the soft thumping of the soldiers' footsteps in the quiet of the corridor. None of the soldiers spoke. I wondered if they would fire without warning. I wondered how long they would let the robot continue to take me away from my prison cell. I wondered why they had let me go this far.

I wondered where I was going. And why.

All I knew was that the robot had appeared as my prison cell door opened, and from the speakers of the robot, a famil-iar but mechanical-sounding voice had instructed me to sit up from my bunk so the robot's arms could lift me. I had trusted that voice.

And now I was here.

With all those neuron rifles ready and able to kill me in the worst way possible.

I didn't even know why I'd been put in this prison. Two days ago, Chase Sanders, my dad and the pilot of the *Moon Racer* spaceship, my friend Ashley, and I had arrived from Mars— where I had been born over 14 Earth years ago. To our shock, World United Federation soldiers had boarded our ship and arrested us. And I hadn't talked to Ashley or my dad since.

In my solitude, I kept wondering if it had anything to do with the robots.

For about as long as I could remember, I had been trained in a virtual-reality program. Like the ones on Earth where you put on a surround-sight helmet that gives you a 3-D view of a scene on a computer program. The helmet is wired so when you turn your head, it directs the computer program to shift the scene as if you were there in real life. Sounds come in like real sounds. Because you're wearing a wired jacket and gloves, the arms and hands you see in your surround-sight picture move wherever you move your own arms and hands.

With me, the only difference is that the wiring reaches my brain directly through my spine. And I can control a real robot, not one in virtual reality. You see, part of the long-term Mars Project that my mom, dad, and I were a part of was to use robots—which don't need oxygen, water, or heat—to explore Mars. However, the problem was that robots couldn't think like humans.

So that's where I came in. When I was a baby, I had an experimental operation to insert a special rod with thousands of tiny, biological implant fibers into my spine. Each of the fibers has a core that transmits impulses of electricity, allowing my brain to control a robot's computer. From all my years of training in a computer simulation program, my mind knows all the muscle moves it takes to handle the virtual-reality controls. Handling the robot is no different, except instead of actually moving my muscles, I imagine I'm moving the muscles. My brain sends the proper nerve impulses to the robot, and it moves the way I made the robot move in the virtual-reality computer program.

I admit, it's cool. Almost worth being in a wheelchair.

Ashley was wired in the same way—with one difference. Because she'd had the operation on Earth, with better medical facilities, her spine hadn't been damaged. She had the best of both worlds.

Now she was controlling the robot that was carrying me.

Only I had no idea how she'd gotten control of it.

Or where we were headed.

Or why.

CHAPTER 2

"Ashley," I whispered to the robot. Somewhere, nearby or far away, my best friend was controlling this robot. "You can see all these soldiers, right?"

It was a dumb question. Of course she could see them. The robot transmitted visuals in four directions through the video lenses perched on top of its body stem. What I was hoping for in Ashley's answer was something that made sense of all the action over the last few minutes.

Especially after endless hours of doing nothing since the arrest except staring at the ceiling and walls of my cell. No one had told me why my father and I were under arrest after our journey from Mars to Earth. No one had even talked to me; the food pushed into my cell came from a surly guard who ignored my questions. And I'd had no idea what had happened to Ashley.

"Yes, I can see the soldiers, Tyce," she answered through the robot's speaker. "If you want, wave at them and smile. They're not going to hurt you. Soon enough, you'll find out why. I can't say anything more. Not in front of them."

She'd spoken loud enough that the nearest soldiers could overhear. I gave a weak smile. If they smiled in return, I couldn't tell. Not with the lights of the corridor bouncing off the mirrored visors of their helmets.

"Ashley?" I took comfort from knowing she was some-where on the other end of the remote X-ray signals that the robot's computer converted to brain-wave signals. I pictured her big grin under the straight, dark hair she kept cut short. At 13, she was a year younger than me. Most of the time she seemed years smarter. Especially in math. "Ashley!"

"Hang on," she answered. "I've got to concentrate on where we're going. I'm using my memory here, and I saw the map only once."

I knew exactly what she meant. Robot control took full concentration. Like her, whenever I handled my own robot, my eyes and ears were cut off from all sight and sound. That allowed me to pay full attention to the information delivered to me from the robot's eyes and ears. It would be no different for Ashley, wherever she was. She'd probably be wearing ear-plugs and some kind of blindfold. It meant that she wouldn't be able to read a map on her end and still maintain control of the robot here.

"If it helps," I said, "it looks like the corridor ends ahead about 25 feet."

"Thanks." The robot continued its steady pace. "I do see it. If I remember, I need to turn left."

Thirty seconds later the robot turned to follow the left branch of the corridor.

The scenery didn't change much. Every 10 feet there was another closed door on each side. The soldiers kept following, their neuron rifles still aimed at my head.

I could hear Ashley count aloud through the robot's voice. "One . . . two . . . three . . . four . . . five . . ."

I realized she was counting doors.

At the 10th door, Ashley stopped and spun the robot's wheels so the robot was facing the door. With me still in its arms.

"Grab the handle," Ashley instructed. "I'd use the robot hands, but I'm afraid of dropping you."

"Sure." I reached out for the handle. The robot held me steady. With the strength in its titanium arms, it could have effortlessly held a person five times my weight.

"Open the door," Ashley directed me. "It should be unlocked."

She was right. The door opened easily. The robot rolled through.

I gasped as the door shut behind us on its automatic hinges.

It was another prison cell. With two men sitting on the bunk. One man held a knife to the other's throat.

The man being held captive I didn't recognize. Wearing an outfit that looked like a one-piece cape, he was elderly and very small. His hair was white, and the wrinkles on his face were deep enough to hold water if he stepped outside in a rainstorm. A slightly worried frown rearranged those wrinkles.

The man holding the knife I did recognize. He was much younger, with square shoulders, a square face, and hair the same color of blond as mine. A big man, wearing a regulation military jumpsuit—like the ones I'd been given during the quarantine process.

This man shifted slightly where he sat on the edge of the bunk, without moving the knife from the older man's throat. He had the older man carefully positioned as a shield, making it risky for the guards to try a neuron shot.

"Hello, Tyce," this man said calmly.

I knew the man holding the knife very well. I had just spent eight months in space with him. "Hello, Dad," I said, cradled helplessly as I was in the robot's arms. "How are you?"

CHAPTER 3

"As a result of this gentleman remaining here with me," Dad said, "the Combat Force commander at this base has agreed to my conditions. Which includes freedom for you and Ashley."

Combat Force. The military arm of the World United Federation.

"He's going to remain with you?" I asked.

The old man did not react to what Dad said. Just sat there patiently, as if it were a regular happening to have someone hold a knife to his throat.

"Just me and Ashley are going?" I didn't know why we had been arrested. I only knew Ashley had been in another prison cell. Dad must have arranged to get her released first. "But what about—?"

"Me? No, Tyce. Say nothing more."

11

By the tone of Dad's voice, I knew I had to obey.

"I wish we could talk freely," Dad continued, "but I have no doubt that this room is under audio surveillance. So don't say anything unless it is a direct reply to one of my questions. Got that?"

"Yes," I said, unfair as it seemed. I had plenty of my own questions that I desperately wanted to ask Dad. Why had we been arrested? Who was this man he held hostage? How had Dad been able to get a knife? What were we going to do about the armed soldiers out in the corridor?

"Tyce," Dad said, "you remember why you and Ashley came back to Earth?"

"Yes."

"When both of you leave here, you must do it. Even without me. Understand?"

Without him? "Dad, I—"

"Answer me with a yes. You will do it without me. Understand?"

"Yes."

"As part of my conditions, you and Ashley will each be equipped with money cards. Don't be afraid to spend what you need because the cards have no limit. Get there and complete the mission. Understand?"

"Yes."

"You have only six days. If you succeed, you can return here for me."

Succeed at what? And if we don't succeed, what will happen to Dad?

"Now carefully reach into my chest pocket. Take the folded piece of paper there. I've written out all the rest of the things I can't say to you here in this cell."

From wherever she was, Ashley moved the robot slowly forward and stopped it just in front of my father.

Two days' worth of beard darkened Dad's face. Half circles of exhaustion showed under his eyes.

"Dad, you all right?" I asked.

He nodded briefly, his lips tight.

The top of the paper showed from his chest pocket. In the robot's arms, I leaned forward. As I did, the old man beside Dad grabbed my lower arm. A sudden sharp pain stabbed my skin.

"Hey!" I yelled.

"Let him go," Dad warned, pressing the knife harder against the old man's throat. I expected to see blood. Instead, I noticed Dad was using the dull side of the knife.

The dull side? It didn't make sense. But I was in no position to comment. Especially with the stabbing pain against the underside of my arm.

"Let him go," Dad said again, his voice growing more intense.

Weird. Dad's voice was louder as if he was angry, but I knew Dad well enough to know when he truly was mad. Who was he trying to fool?

Finally the old man released my arm.

I looked at my skin and saw blood. How had the old man managed to break skin? So many questions. And none that I could ask.

"Tyce," Dad ordered, "take the note. Time matters a great deal. When you read it, you'll understand why."

I ignored the tiny drops of blood on my arm, pulled the paper loose from Dad's chest pocket, and slipped it into my own pocket. The robot backed away, holding me safely.

"I have also arranged for you and Ashley to have a radio linked by satellite to a radio that will be provided to me," Dad said. "Use it to speak to me only when necessary. Remember, we need to keep our communications to a minimum, because I'm sure we will be monitored. Also remember it's important that you report to me every half hour." He smiled grimly as he continued. "Without those reports, this gentleman here is in serious trouble."

The old man's frown deepened.

"You are his lifeline," Dad explained to my puzzled look. "As long as I know you are safe, he is safe. If they send any-one after you, if they stop you in any way—"

"No need to explain," the old man interrupted. He hadn't said a word to this point, and the calm deepness of his voice was a surprise. "If the kids get hurt, I get hurt. The Combat Force commander knows this very clearly. All your conditions have been met. But I warn you now—their deaths will be in your hands."

"If anyone in the Combat Force harms them—," Dad began.

"It won't be the Force that kills them, you young fool."

I'd never heard anyone speak to my father this way. More surprisingly, Dad accepted the rebuke. Who was this old man?

"Sending them out into the swamps of the Everglades will kill them as surely as any military command," the old man went on.

Everglades?

"And furthermore, young man," he told Dad, "exactly how long do you think you can stay awake?"

Dad didn't answer. At least not to the old man. "Tyce," Dad replied, "he's right. All I can guarantee you for a head start is the length of time that I can sit here. When I fall asleep . . ."

He didn't have to finish that thought. I understood. When Dad fell asleep and the knife fell from his hand, he'd no longer have a hostage.

"I won't leave you," I blurted. "Send Ashley by herself. I'll help you. We can take turns staying awake and keeping him hostage while she—"

"Go," Dad insisted. "Later, when you read the note, you'll understand." He gave me a look I couldn't interpret.

"No."

"You'll have to trust me," Dad said gently. "I'm your father."

"No," I said. "I won't leave you."

"You have no choice."

Dad lifted his eyes from mine and stared directly into the front video lens of the robot that held me. "Ashley, take him away."

The robot began to roll back toward the door, with me still helpless in its arms.

"No!" I shouted at the robot. "Ashley, let me stay!"

My desperate plea did no good.

The last view I had of my father was of him sitting on the bunk. With a solemn expression on his face.

"You need to succeed, Tyce. You have six days. And the countdown begins now."

CHAPTER 4

With soldiers following, the robot approached the main doors of the Combat Force's prison.

I now knew why they had not fired any shots from their neuron rifles. Dad was protecting me by holding that old man hostage. But only for as long as he could remain awake.

At that instant I hated like I'd never hated before. I hated the fact that I was being carried. I hated the fact that the operation on my spine had left me without the use of my legs. I hated the fact I couldn't get to my feet and charge back to the prison cell. That I couldn't help the father I used to dislike and had only recently come to understand. I couldn't lose him now—especially when he'd also become my friend.

But I was helpless. As the robot rolled forward I didn't even bother pleading with Ashley anymore. A few feet later

I heard Mom's voice in my mind. *"Tyce, we just have to trust God. Even when things look bad, he's got everything under control."* She'd said it before, and she'd been right. But what about this time? Although I, too, had come to believe in and trust God, this situation looked impossible. How was God going to fix this?

Now the doors to the outside loomed in front of me. Despite my anger and fear, I began to feel excitement. Like opening a present on Christmas, except a thousand times stronger.

It had been night when Dad, Ashley, and I and the rest of the crew of the *Moon Racer* had been shuttled from orbit to Earth. We had landed at this military base, and the shuttle had coasted into a large warehouse. On the ground we'd been transferred through a chute from the shuttle into an electric vehicle that took us deeper into the base. Finally we'd reached the prison area after a brief time in quarantine. Not once during the process had I seen anything of the Earth's surface. I had not even gulped one breath of outside air.

And now?

When the doors in front of me opened, I'd be somewhere I had dreamed about for years. Ever since understanding that I was the only person in the entire solar system to be born off the planet Earth.

Yes, I'd be outside, without a space suit. On Earth. Breathing in open air, outside of buildings. For the first time in my life. As the main doors swung open to the outside, I sucked a big lungful of air and held my breath.

The next instant I lost all that air. For what I saw took my breath away.

Blue sky!

Yellow sun!

White clouds!

On Mars, the landscape was a butterscotch-colored sky with a blue sun and orange clouds. I'd only ever read or seen on DVD-gigarom how things looked on Earth. This was far more beautiful than I'd ever imagined.

In that moment, I forgot about my dad. I forgot about the six-day countdown. I forgot about the impossible mission of rescue that Ashley and I faced.

Blue sky!

Yellow sun!

White clouds!

And heat. Wonderful warmth on my skin. With air moving across me.

I drew in another lungful of breath—just because it was so sweet to drink in this fresh air.

The ground was black and smooth in front of me. This was the end of the runway that the shuttle had landed on when we'd been taken here. A few different airplanes—which I recognized from movies I had watched on Mars—were parked at the side of this runway. To my left and to my right were the buildings of the military base, including the large, tall bay that the shuttle had parked in. All of this looked like an island set in the middle of the swamps that surrounded it.

As the robot rolled closer to the edge of the runway, I was overwhelmed by smells that came with the air I drank in so greedily. I was used to a landscape of frozen brown and red desert, long sucked dry of any hint of moisture. Here? Beyond the parking lot was a wall of green. Tall plants reaching for the sky. Small plants crowding the bases of the large plants. With colorful blossoms that gave incredible smells. Wow! Wow! *Wow!*

And noises! The creaking and buzzing and twittering of living things that swarmed in the green plants at the edge of the parking lot.

This was Earth! How incredible.

"Tyce? Tyce?" Ashley's voice broke through.

"I can hear you," I finally answered.

"It's okay," she said. "Really, it's okay."

I didn't answer her. I was still trying to comprehend all of this. *This is really Earth!*

"We'll get through this," Ashley promised through the robot's speakers. "In less than a week, you'll see your dad again. We'll make sure of it."

I suddenly realized why she was trying to reassure me. Because I suddenly realized I was crying, and the sound of it must have reached her. She didn't know I wasn't crying because of my dad. But because of how beautiful God's creation was. *Earth!*

"A-Ashley," I stuttered, "I . . . I . . ." I couldn't finish. I couldn't find any words to express what it felt like to be outside, under the blue sky of Earth, for the first time in my life. Instead, I turned my eyes to the sky and thought, *Wow, God. Thanks.*

"Hang on," Ashley said. "I'll have you with me right away. I'm here. At the edge of the runway. In this boat."

I noticed for the first time that the trees in front of me weren't a solid wall. In the gap, I saw a large boat. With what looked like a giant fan mounted on the back. At the front of it stood a man, his hands on a steering wheel. At the back was a canvas roof propped by four poles, one in each corner.

"Airboat," Ashley said, reading the question in my mind. "For riding the top of the shallow water of the Everglades."

I remembered what the old man had said in Dad's prison cell. *"Sending them out into the swamps of the Everglades will kill them as surely as any military command."*

We were going out there? Into all those trees and plants and among all those strange noises of all that hidden, buzzing life? On water?

Suddenly the familiar, barren, frozen desert of the Martian landscape seemed like a very safe home.

CHAPTER 5

A heavy rumbling noise came from the airboat's motor.

The robot rolled up a ramp onto the boat. Below the ramp was dark water that smelled strange to my accustomed-to-Mars nostrils.

Water! The boat rested in a channel hundreds of yards long that finally disappeared in the distance among the trees and vegetation.

I could hardly comprehend so much water out in the open. On Mars, water was as precious as electricity and oxygen, and it was guarded and recycled as if our lives depended on it. Which, of course, they did.

Yet here was water, in the open, and more of it than I'd seen in my entire life. I might have stopped to stare with an open jaw, but the robot reached the top of the ramp and rolled into the boat.

The 20 soldiers with the neuron rifles remained at the edge of the parking lot until we had boarded. Then they lowered their rifles and turned to leave, walking in tight formation in their black uniforms.

The soldier behind the wheel at the front of the boat wore an identical uniform and had the standard, clipped-short hair. His tan face showed no expression. Nor did he say anything.

I ignored him in return. My attention was on Ashley.

She sat at the back of the boat, propped by seat cushions to stay upright, since her own body was basically helpless as she controlled the robot. She wore a blindfold and a headset. Around the waist of her military jumpsuit was a robot pack, which is a mini-transmitter. It was the "bot-pack" that made my rescue possible. All my life on Mars, I'd worked in a laboratory under the dome, hooked into a large computer system that was definitely not portable. When Ashley had arrived on Mars, she'd brought the next generation of robot-control technology—the bot-pack, a mobile robot-control package that hung on a belt.

"Welcome, Martian," the robot said to me.

Good old Ashley. Making a joke about my origins. "Hello, earthling," I fired back.

It was weird. Ashley was only a couple of steps away

from me, under the shade of the canvas roof. Yet she wasn't seeing me with her eyes but through the robot's video lenses. She didn't speak to me with her voice but through the robot's speakers. Only after she disengaged from the robot would the reverse happen. The robot would become lifeless, and then Ashley would use her own body to see me and talk to me.

"Don't think being so friendly is going to help," I said. "That's my father you made me leave behind in there. I—"

"You need to get into your wheelchair," she interrupted. "It's an older model but all they could come up with here on short notice. Once you're in it, you can yell at me all you want."

A wheelchair was parked beside Ashley. Not the one I'd taken with me from Mars but a bigger one, with an electric motor. Another full-size robot stood beside it. A bot-pack hung from the left handle of the wheelchair. A backpack hung from the other handle.

"No," I said stubbornly. "Once I get into the wheel-chair, this boat will leave, won't it? And my father will be by himself."

"In two more minutes when I get a chance to talk to you," Ashley reasoned through the robot's speakers, "all of this will be clear. Let me disengage from the robot, so I can explain to you what I know. Your dad's note will do the rest. But I don't want to treat you like a baby and force you into the wheelchair. Please?"

Finally I nodded.

The robot moved the extra few feet to the wheelchair and gently lowered me into place. The boat rocked in the water at the shifting of our weight.

"All right," I said as the robot backed away. "I'm ready."

The robot parked itself beside the other robot. It lowered its arms. Shutters dropped to protect the video lenses. I knew what Ashley was doing because of the countless times I had done it myself. Disengaging from the robot controls by shouting *"Stop!"* in her mind.

A second later Ashley pulled off her headset and blindfold. She blinked against the brightness of the sun and pushed back her straight, black hair. The sun highlighted her cheekbones, beautiful dark eyes, and Asian features. When Ashley grinned, she looked her age. But when she frowned, people stepped back. She appeared grown-up enough to be intimidating.

This time she neither grinned nor frowned but gave me a gentle smile. "Hey, Tyce. It's good to see you."

It was good to see her too. But I was still mad enough that I didn't want to say it.

Before I could think of something else to say instead, she raised her voice and spoke to the soldier at the front of the boat. "We're ready. Take us away."

The motor roared, the giant fan blades began to whir, and we shot forward in the water.

CHAPTER 6

In one way, Ashley was immediately wrong.

Despite her promise, she wasn't able to tell me much in the next two minutes. Not with the roar of the motor and the fan blades. Wind whipped my face and my hair, a sensation I loved. I had never felt anything like it.

The boat rocked and shook as it sped down the flat water of the channel.

Ashley squatted beside me and moved her face close to my ear. "Like I said before, most boats have propellers! But that would never get us through the Everglades. We'll have to put up with the noise for a couple of hours!"

"Where are we going?"

"To the western edge of the Everglades. They've arranged for a helicopter to take us from there."

"Why not just have the helicopter pick us up at the base," I yelled back.

"Good question," she answered. "I've wondered myself."

"What if we get lost?" I shouted. It had taken less than 30 seconds for the channel to take us deep into the thick vegetation. It was as if the Combat Force base no longer existed.

"GPS," she said. "Same as on Mars."

I nodded. Satellites that orbited Mars fed signals to handheld global positioning units, making it possible to pinpoint your location on a grid of the planet.

The boat swung violently to make a turn. I clutched the arms of my wheelchair. I was glad someone had tied it to the side to keep it from rolling.

Ashley toppled over. When she recovered, she squatted beside me again. "I'm going to sit at the side of the boat. In the meantime, read your dad's note."

Instead of shouting again, I simply nodded.

I reached into my pocket, opened the note, and began to read.

Tyce,

There is much that confuses me about all of this. What I can guess comes from the questions I was asked by Combat Force officials since we landed on Earth. It seems that although Dr. Jordan is high up in Combat Force command, no one in the World United Federation government or the Combat Force knew about Dr. Jordan's project with Ashley and the others. It appears, as a secret agent for the rebel force Terratakers, he has run this project without authorization. Nor, somehow, does anyone know about the recent events on Mars, including the hostage taking under the dome or the Hammerhead testing. It's as if all communications from Mars to Earth over the last eight months were silenced without the knowledge of anyone on Mars. My guess is that Luke Daab controlled all communications by computer, just as he did on the Moon Racer.

Dr. Jordan's last communication from the Moon Racer was that we had abandoned him in outer space to kill him. He wanted it to look like he was dead and at the same time cast suspicion on us. That was the reason we were initially arrested.

I have said nothing about him surviving, simply because I didn't know if I could trust anybody, not until finally talking with the supreme governor. I'm now glad I said so little to the Combat Force people here.

Because of the robots on our ship and the other equipment, they are very curious about you and Ashley. Two of the highest generals in the Combat Force are scheduled to arrive this afternoon to oversee experiments on you and Ashley. It was imperative that you both escape before that happened. Once they understand what you are capable of doing, they will want to use you in the same ways that Dr. Jordan intended. As military weapons.

Also, you know Dr. Jordan ejected from the Moon Racer in an escape pod. At this point, he has no reason to think his plan to destroy the Moon Racer failed. As you also know, he has already arrived, but as far as I can tell, he has kept this hidden from his Combat Force connections. It wasn't until meeting with the supreme governor that I learned what he has been doing since reaching Earth and what he intends.

This is the second reason you and Ashley needed to escape immediately. Once Jordan knows you are still alive, he will try to capture you, and failing that, send someone to kill you. I'm sure Jordan would prefer to see you dead than let the World United Federation truly understand the scope of his project. After all, he still has the other kids under his control—for as long as the Federation does not discover their existence.

No one on an official level in the Federation or the Combat Force knows about Dr. Jordan and the others except you and me and Ashley. When the generals arrive, I am sure they will ask me about you two, especially after Ashley demonstrated her control of a robot by rescuing you. They will not, however, have any reason to suspect there are others. Or that I know there are others.

You and Ashley, then, must keep their existence secret as you try to find a way to stop Dr. Jordan. Trust no one unless they prove I have sent them. You must also reach the other kids before Dr. Jordan or the Combat Force does. If possible, get them to a place where the media can report them. Once the world knows of them, they will no longer be considered a secret weapon. And they, along with you, will finally be safe. Once that happens, the Combat Force will have no reason to keep me prisoner.

If you don't have time to reach the media, you need to find a way to stop Dr. Jordan. I can't stress this enough. Stop him even if it means my death.

Also, immediately get rid of the radio. I only referred you to it for the sake of the listening device. It may have a tracking device. Don't worry about sending back reports. I have arranged another way to follow your progress. Nor do you need to worry about me. I have no intention of harming my hostage. In fact, I will be releasing him before the afternoon is over. In turn, he will make sure I come to no harm,

*at least for the next six days while you get proof for the world
about Jordan's secret program. You see, this man is . . .*

Dad's words reached the end of the front of the page.
I stopped for a second, wondering about the last paragraph.
For the sake of the listening device. How much had been said
in there that I misunderstood? I sure hoped I was about to
get the rest of the answers. I began to turn the page to read
the rest.

A sudden drop in noise, however, distracted me. The boat's
engine began to sputter, and the fan blades lost their power.

Just as suddenly, the engine quit and the sputtering
ended completely.

Ashley darted forward beside me. I folded the note and
put it back in my pocket. What was going on?

The boat began to coast toward the edge of the channel.
Blades of long grass slapped at the hull.

"The radio," I told Ashley. "Get on the radio and let Dad
know what's happened." He had told me to get rid of it, but
I thought he'd at least want to know about this new develop-
ment. After that, I'd throw it overboard.

"Sure," Ashley said. "I'll—"

Our pilot screamed and fell over. He lay, shaking out
of control, on the floor of the boat. His feet thumped a wild
drumming pattern.

Only one thing could have done that to him. A neuron rifle! But who and where?

Movement ahead answered my question. A low, flat boat glided silently out of the vegetation, where it evidently had been waiting in ambush. A man stood at the front, holding with both hands a long pole that stuck into the ground beneath the water. He leaned into the pole, and the boat moved closer. He pulled it loose, lifted it, stuck it into the ground again, and leaned, repeating this quickly until he was almost at our own boat.

It was then that I saw the neuron rifle behind him on the seat of the flat boat.

But only Combat Force soldiers are authorized to have neuron rifles, I thought. *And even then, a neuron rifle doesn't work unless its internal computer chip reads a fingerprint pattern belonging to an authorized user.*

This man, in his tattered dark clothing, definitely did not look military. Nor did he look like an authorized user.

He grinned wildly, his teeth shining brightly beneath a greasy, wide-brimmed hat. He had a big, bushy black beard and equally bushy long hair. A large knife was strapped on a belt around his waist.

"Come in!" Ashley shouted into the radio behind me. "Come in. We're under attack."

The other boat was much lower in the water than ours. The wild man stared upward into my eyes. He kept grinning.

"You can tell her the radio won't work." He took one

hand off his pushing pole and pointed to a small black box beside the neuron rifle on the seat of the boat. "This little gadget jams any electrical signals for 100 yards in any direction. It's how I got your boat engine to quit. And it's why no one can hear your friend, no matter how loud she yells into her radio."

He grabbed a rope and put the end of it in his mouth. With clenched jaws and both hands free, he took hold of the edge of our boat to pull himself in. With a grunt and a quickness that surprised me in a man so large, he rolled over the edge and landed feetfirst in our boat.

"Don't try anything stupid," he said as he spit out the rope in his mouth. The other end of the rope was tied to his flat-bottom boat. With quick movements of nimble fingers, he tied this end to our boat, securing both boats together. "Make this easy on me. And I promise you won't get hurt."

CHAPTER 7

The wild man took a short piece of rope out of his pocket and stepped toward Ashley. "Drop the radio. Give me your hands."

Ashley threw me the radio.

"Give me your hands," he repeated.

"No." Ashley kicked him in the shins.

He laughed. "Really. I don't want to hurt you. Let's get this over with."

She tried kicking him again, but he had reached out and placed his right palm on her forehead. She couldn't reach him, hard as she tried.

The laughter left his voice. "Young woman, there is no place for you to go. You wouldn't be able to swim 50 yards before a gator got you."

"No, no, no," Ashley said. "If you really aren't going to hurt us, you wouldn't try to tie my hands."

"You're worth a lot of money if I deliver you safely, and that's what I intend to—," the wild man began. He had all but ignored me, assuming, I'm sure, that just because I was in a wheelchair I was useless. But as Ashley kicked at him, he backed up, almost to my legs.

In that second I threw the radio overboard. Then I pushed upward off the handles of my wheelchair and managed to wrap my arms around his neck.

The wild man grunted again, this time with surprise. He clawed at my arms, trying to pull me free.

I had no muscle control over my legs, but since I'd spent a lifetime using my arms to push my wheelchair around, I had far more strength in my upper body than most people guessed. Big and strong as this wild man was, he wasn't able to shake me loose.

He began to thrash around as I choked the air from his windpipe. I just wanted him unconscious. Ashley punched him in the stomach.

"Aaarrgh!" He thrashed harder, then moved to the side of the boat. Before I could react, he spun around so that I was hanging from his neck and shoulders above the water. "Aaarrgh!"

He was fading. I could tell by the way his attempts to

yank my arms loose got weaker and weaker. But if he fell backward . . .

And that's exactly what happened. My weight pulled him toward the water, and he toppled out of the boat. With me clinging to his neck. Together we fell into the side of the flat-bottom boat.

There was a horrible thunk as his head slammed into the wood, and in the next instant, we hit water.

In shock, I let go. I gasped and water choked me. Panicked, I splashed frantically with my arms. The most water that had ever surrounded me was the fine spray of a shower on Mars. I had no idea how to swim, yet somehow my splashing kept my head above water. My eyes cleared, and I saw the side of the flat-bottom boat above me. I jabbed one hand upward, and my fingers closed on the edge. It gave me enough leverage to pull up with the other hand.

The flat-bottom boat tilted toward me as I clung to the side. The neuron rifle and black box slid toward me.

With my body weight supported by the water, I was able to pull halfway out. But that was it. I couldn't get any more of my body into the boat.

"Tyce!" Ashley shouted. "Tyce! Help me roll him over."

Out of the corner of my eye, I saw a flash. Ashley had used the boat hook to reach down for us. Holding to the side of the boat, my legs dangling uselessly in the water, I turned my head.

Ashley had managed to get the hook into the wild man's clothing. But he floated facedown. Blood streamed into the water from where he'd hit his skull.

Clinging to the flat-bottom boat with one arm, I reached for the wild man with the other. I grabbed a limp arm and rolled him over. Ashley worked the hook loose and then hooked his belt to support most of his weight. With one hand I held his head above the water. With the other arm I clung to the boat.

"I'm not sure how long I can hold him," I groaned. With his weight dragging on me, my armpit was already numb.

I looked up at Ashley. She stood at the side of the boat, leaning over, holding the boat-hook pole with both hands as she kept the wild man from sinking. Her eyes were focused beyond me, however, and her jaw had opened in shock.

"Hold him, Tyce. Just for a couple of seconds." She disappeared from view.

I couldn't turn my head to see what she'd seen. Without the support of her boat hook, the wild man's weight doubled. I nearly collapsed, and the flat-bottom boat tilted even more dangerously toward us.

A second later she was back, with the wild man's neuron rifle. She pointed it beyond me and the boat.

"What is it?" I shouted.

"You don't want to know!"

I saw her trigger finger pull several times.

"What is it?" I shouted again. "The rifle isn't programmed for you! It won't shoot!"

"Alligator. And it's headed right for the both of you!"

CHAPTER 8

Alligator!

I'd seen them but only on the DVD-gigaroms on computer screens. Growing up on Mars, I'd spent endless hours learning everything I could about Earth. Earth animals fascinated me, and some of my favorite clips had been of the giant predators. Lions, tigers, sharks. And, of course, alligators.

My mouth instantly went dry with fear.

Alligator! I knew it didn't bite its prey to death. No, it pulled the prey underwater—a person, deer, anything too large to swallow—and spun it underwater in circles until it drowned. Then it found an underwater log and jammed the dead prey into place until it had rotted soft enough to tear apart.

I didn't want that prey to be me.

Frantically, I turned my head, straining until it felt like my neck would snap.

And I saw it.

Like a giant log, but with an evil, narrowing snout, it approached slowly. It was probably drawn by the sound of our thrashing in the water or maybe by the smell of the wild man's blood. Its eyes were barely above the water. Its tail twisted the surface of the water with powerful, snakelike thrusts.

"Ashley," I gasped. "Jump into the lower boat!"

She understood immediately. That was our only chance. That she stand in the flat boat and haul us in from there.

When she landed, the flat-bottom boat swayed danger-ously, but it was low enough and wide enough to give the stability she needed. She grabbed my shoulder and began to pull me upward.

The wild man was still unconscious. "No," I said. "Him first."

Ashley tugged him by the hair, bringing him close enough to grab his shoulders. She leaned way back in the boat to get her weight on the far side. With my free hand I held his shirt and pushed.

He was too heavy. It wasn't going to work.

I twisted my head. The gator was about 10 seconds away!

"Try harder!" I shouted.

The wild man coughed and sputtered. His eyes opened wide. For a split second, I stared into his startlingly blue eyes.

"Gator!" I shouted at him. "Get in!"

He looked past me and saw the gator.

Seven seconds away.

He gripped the side of the boat. Then, with his other hand, he grabbed the back of my jumpsuit. With a heave of his other huge arm, he flung me over the edge of the boat.

I landed hard with my chin on the seat of the boat. Stunned. Water streamed from my jumpsuit.

I pushed up on my arms. My face bumped into the little black box that he had used to jam the electrical signals.

The gator was almost on the wild man.

His hand came out of the water with his knife. He lifted it high.

The gator's mouth opened wide, showing yellow, jagged teeth and the pink, soft inside of its throat.

And as the thought entered my mind, I acted. I picked up the little black box and fired it into that wide-open mouth.

The jaws snapped shut.

The gator roared! It flipped over and thrashed from side to side.

The wild man screamed at the same time. He began to sink in the water. Ashley grabbed his arm and held him to the side of the boat. She, too, screamed.

Then it was over. The gator sank. And Ashley and the wild man gasped for breath.

"You felt that too?" he said to Ashley.

She nodded. "A shock when I touched you."

"Trust me," he said, recovering his breath. "It was worse on me. I was in the water. And it's a great conductor of electricity." His massive chest heaved against the fabric of his wet shirt. Then, out of the blue, he began to laugh. "If electricity from the black box was shocking you and me, think of what it was doing to that gator." He wiped blood from his forehead. Water dripped from his matted beard. The wild man directed his next words at me. "When that gator was coming, you could have got into the boat first."

"Maybe," I answered. I felt dumb lying on my stomach in the boat, my head resting on the seat, peering upward like some baby crawling on the floor. So I pulled myself up by my arms and rolled over to a sitting position. My jumpsuit was squishy with water. A few strands of green weed clung to my chest. "But I would have had to let go of you first. I was afraid you'd sink."

"Which means you saved my life." The wild man shook his head. Blood kept dribbling down into his eyebrows. He must have had a cut hidden somewhere under his thick hair. "Actually, twice. Because you zapped the gator with the black box. I'm not sure my knife would have done much good against that monster."

He grinned, and his teeth flashed white against his dark, wet beard. "I guess I owe you then. That changes things so completely that I don't have much choice but to go on the run. With you." He shook his head. "Plus you just cost me a million dollars."

"Pardon me?"

"I'll explain later. We've got less than five minutes to clear this area. Or all of us are dead."

As if in answer to him, we heard the roar of boat motors in the distance.

He got to his feet. The flat-bottom boat wobbled as he stepped toward our bigger boat and hauled himself into it. Moving quickly to the front, the wild man lifted the unconscious pilot and dragged him to the edge above us.

"Sounds like them," he said. "Help me get this guy down into the flat-bottom. Because now I'd say we have less than two minutes."

CHAPTER 9

"My name is Nate!" he shouted above the noise of the engine. "Guys in the platoon called me Wild Man. Ashley and Tyce, right?"

With effortless efficiency, he had already lifted Ashley up from the flat-bottom boat into our boat. He'd done the same with me, setting me into my wheelchair as if gravity didn't exist for us. Next he'd moved forward and restarted the engine.

"Right," Ashley answered. She gave me a strange look. I could guess what she was thinking. *How does he know our names?*

I expected Nate to get us out of here immediately. Instead, he knelt by the dash of the boat and reached underneath. When he pulled his hand back, I saw a small gray box, with some wires dangling from where he had ripped it loose.

"Tracking device," Nate shouted. "Now they'll have to find us the old-fashioned way."

Tracking device? How could he know about that, too?

Nate threw the tracking device into the flat-bottom boat, where the pilot was just beginning to wake up from the neuron blast.

"Adios!" Nate yelled at the pilot, then slammed the controls into forward. The boat shot ahead into the channel.

He knew our names. He knew about the hidden tracking device. He'd known where to wait in ambush. He'd been supplied a neuron rifle by someone from the Federation's Combat Force.

Was there an explanation for this on the back of Dad's note to me?

I had a sudden sick feeling. *The note! The note in my pocket!* I'd fallen into the water. What would be left of it?

The boat lurched. I managed to snap open my chest pocket. All I was able to extract was a soggy wad of useless paper.

What had I missed? What had been on the other side of the note to guide Ashley and me? I leaned back in my wheelchair, angry and frustrated.

Nate maneuvered the boat at top speed, throwing Ashley and me from side to side as we followed the twists of the channel farther and farther into the swamp.

Then I watched with horror as he gunned the boat to even higher speeds on the next straight stretch. Ahead was a turn, but there was no way we'd make it at this speed.

The boat charged forward, directly toward a wall of trees and high swamp grass.

Impact in less than three seconds!

Two!

One!

Bang! The front of the boat hit the shallow bank of land.

The impact threw me out of the wheelchair. If the brakes hadn't been set and if the wheelchair hadn't been tied in place, the force would have thrown the wheelchair into the front of the boat.

We were airborne!

I clenched my jaw, waiting for a bigger bang as the boat slammed into solid ground.

The boat motor still roared as the seconds seemed to stretch into a lifetime.

Splash! Nate had found a large open area of water on the other side of the land, screened by the vegetation, with a new channel visible at the far end.

Briefly Nate turned back to us from the steering wheel at the front of the boat. "That should lose them. So settle back and enjoy the ride. We've got about another two hours ahead of us."

I couldn't help the thought that flashed through my mind. *And then what?*

CHAPTER 10

The three of us sat in front of a small fire on a small island. The grass was packed down to make sitting more comfortable for Nate and Ashley. (The good thing about being in a wheelchair is that you always have a place to sit.) There were a few large trees with roots visible above the ground, so it looked like they were resting on giant claws.

Three hours had passed since we had left the pilot behind in the flat-bottom boat. Two and a half of those hours we'd spent twisting and turning through the Everglades. Sometimes on open water, sometimes through channels, and often it seemed we were riding tall grass as the boat skimmed in shallow water.

It had been an incredible two and a half hours for me. The first part of the ride my mind had been full of questions chasing questions. When I'd finally realized that I had no hope of answering those questions without more information, I'd forced myself to think of other things. Like the sky and the wind and the smells and the sights.

For the rest of the boat ride, I had simply stared around me in amazement, trying to match what I saw in the Everglades with what I remembered from the DVD-gigaroms I had watched all my life on Mars. The boat startled large white birds with long, skinny legs, sending them clumsily into the air. I saw turtles sunning on logs. Dozens of kinds of tiny, colorful birds. Trees that were draped with long, dark moss, so that they looked like hunched-over old women.

Again and again I marveled at the new sights and smells. When Nate finally stopped the boat and cut the engine, I was able to hear bird cries and insects buzzing and the splash of fish jumping.

Amazing, I told myself again and again. How could any-one live in all this and not believe someone created it? *Just amazing,* I thought, awed. I envied all the people who had grown up on Earth—which meant everyone in the solar sys-tem except for me—because they were able to see stuff like this every day of their lives.

I had mentioned how cool I thought Earth was—and everything on it—to Nate when he first helped me out of the boat and set me up in the wheelchair on dry land. He'd given me a strange look, followed by a smile. He said he would be happy to discuss that later but needed to get us supper first.

Then he had disappeared for 15 minutes, returning with three fish, each a little bigger than one of his large hands.

As he started a fire, I watched an insect with wings land on the inside of my arm, just above the place where the old man had jabbed me and left a small scab of drying blood. The insect seemed so delicate, I marveled that it could fly.

I felt a tiny pinprick. Had this tiny thing actually bitten me? I kept watching the insect. It began to swell.

"What are you doing?" Nate the wild man asked me. "Slap it. It's sucking your blood."

"Acck!" I slapped it. Blood spread across my arm.

"What planet are you from?" he joked. "Haven't you seen a mosquito before?"

So that's what the little flying thing was. A mosquito. I'd read about them. I sure wasn't going to tell this man why I didn't know what it was. Dad's note had urged strict secrecy. From everyone.

Nate threw me a small can. "Spray this repellent on yourself. As the sun sets, they'll come out in droves."

"Thanks," I said.

"Thank me by trading with me," he answered.

"Trading?" Ashley echoed. "What do Tyce and I have that we can trade?"

"We'll trade information." Nate knelt beside the fish

he had dropped on the grass. "You tell me things. I tell you things. Simple, right?" He yanked loose his huge knife from his belt.

"Easy for you to say when you've got the knife," I told him. "Plus, you're easily 30 years old. I'm only 14 and in a wheelchair. At this point I'd be dumb to disagree with you."

Nate laughed. "Thirty-two. Which has nothing to do with this knife. Because you don't understand. The way I was raised, a man pays his debts. You saved my life twice. From here on I'm your protection. And from what little I can figure, you're going to need it."

He picked up one of the fish and held it upside-down. With a quick movement, he slit the fish's belly from the tail to its gills. He reached into the fish and pulled out a stringy clump of gleaming, colored tubes.

"What's that?" I asked. I was torn between two curiosities. What he'd meant by what he'd said. And what I was seeing.

"Fish guts," he said. "How can you be as old as you are and not know that?"

He must not know I've grown up on Mars, I thought.

Ashley poked the guts with her finger. "Hmm." She had spent a lot of her life in a secret institute. Evidently this was new to her, too. She sniffed her finger and made a face.

It took less than a minute for Nate to take the guts out of the other fish too. He left the guts in a neat pile beside him. "Dinnertime," he announced.

"People eat fish guts?" I asked, startled. I could smell them from where I sat. I didn't know if I was that hungry just yet.

Another strange look from Nate. "Where *exactly* are you from? Mars or something?" He chuckled, then punched me on the shoulder.

I shrugged as an answer. I doubted he'd believe me anyway.

"I save those to use as bait to catch a turtle or two," Nate said. "Turtle soup tastes great. And you can boil and eat it right out of its shell. God's made it an animal that provides its own bowl."

Nate rose and rinsed the gutted fish in the water beside us. He stopped at a bush and cut loose a green branch. "See. This is our frying pan."

He poked the branch through one of the fish and held it above the fire. "Now, while these fish cook, let's talk."

CHAPTER 11

"I've got some questions, then," I said. The smell of the roasting fish made my mouth water. I wondered what "real food" would taste like. That was the kind of thing you could never experience on DVD-gigarom. Sure, I'd had a few meals in the prison. But they had been pretty tasteless, just like the nutrient tubes I'd had all my life on Mars. The only difference was that the prison meals had been served on a tin plate rather than in a tube.

"I'll give you what answers I can," Nate replied. The fire popped and sent ashes and sparks upward, hitting him in the chest. He absently wiped the ash off. I now understood why his clothes smelled the way they did—wild and smoky.

"You had a neuron rifle programmed to allow you to shoot our pilot. I don't think you're a soldier. Even if you somehow stole or found the rifle, it takes a Combat Force computer to program it for you. Which means someone high up arranged it for you. So I'd like to know who gave you the rifle."

I stopped long enough to try the fish. Nate had instructed me to peel the meat back from the skin so I wouldn't eat any scales. As promised, the white meat fell from the bones. With hesitation, I placed some in my mouth.

Wow! I'd never tasted anything so good in my entire life on Mars!

Nate smiled at my reaction. "More questions?"

I nodded but ate all my fish first, then licked my fingers clean. "All right. How did you know our names? How did you know there was a tracking device on board and where it was? How did you know we were going to be coming down that channel at that time? How did you get the little black box to jam the electrical currents?"

Ashley jumped in. "You knew there would be boats chasing us. How? How did you know where to escape? What did you mean when you said Tyce cost you a million dollars? And that now all three of us would be on the run?"

"And," I added, "you said you guessed we needed protection. What made you guess that?"

"You mean aside from the obvious?" he responded, grinning. "That you've escaped a Combat Force prison on the space base?"

"How could you even know that?" Ashley asked him. "Unless someone told you ahead of time. So who was that?"

"Even if someone didn't tell me," Nate returned, "there are the prison uniforms that are too large for each of you. Before you fall asleep tonight, I'll give you the clothes I got for you. You can change, and we'll burn the prison outfits."

"So you did know ahead of time," Ashley said.

"Yup." Nate took his knife out of his sheath again. I hoped he meant what he said about protecting us.

He slid the knife under the fish on the branch. With the fish balanced on the blade, he handed it to Ashley. "Eat carefully. I'd hate to see you burn your fingers or your tongue."

Nate propped the next fish on a branch so it would begin to cook. Ashley prayed quietly before she ate.

"I never used to do that myself," he said, waiting respectfully until she finished before he spoke. "But after a few years here in the swamps, I've learned a whole new appreciation for the nature of creation."

A few years in the swamps? No wonder it seemed like he was as comfortable living in the dangerous wildness of the Everglades as I had been living under the dome on Mars.

"I'll get to your questions first," he said next. "Most all of them are answered by telling you how I knew you'd be on this swamp boat on that channel when you were. But my answer is going to lead to my own questions, so be ready to return the favor."

I wasn't going to make promises, so I kept my mouth shut. Ashley was too busy eating to speak.

"As you might guess," Nate said, "I live here in the Everglades. About five years ago, I retired from the Combat Force. I was so tired of the fighting and the politics and the way the world was going that I decided I was done with it. So I ran—as far away from everything as I could. This natural preserve was as far away and wild as I could get."

Ashley spit some fish bones out, then smiled an apology at me.

"Yesterday, at the cabin I'd built 50 miles from the nearest road, my former commander dropped in on me. Literally. By helicopter. Turns out I hadn't hidden myself as well as I thought. But then I was a fool to believe they wouldn't keep track of me. Not after the kinds of jobs I'd been given during my military service. I used to be part of an elite commando group. We'd be sent into places when the government wanted a problem solved quickly and quietly. . . ." His voice trailed off and he stared into the fire.

It didn't seem like the kind of silence to interrupt. I gazed above him at the late-afternoon sky. The smudged clouds glowed with pinks, reds, and purples as the setting sun bounced light off them.

"Cannon—"

Ashley interrupted. "Cannon?"

"My former commander," Nate explained. "I was part of an elite platoon of the Combat Force. Called the EAGLES."

"Eagles?" I asked. "You flew?"

"EAGLES. I won't even try to explain what it stands for. In short, we were trained to fly anything, pilot any kind of boat, drive any vehicle. We were experts in things that now give me nightmares. Everything. Cannon is no longer in the EAGLES platoon. He's now one of the top-ranking generals in the Combat Force. Imagine my surprise when he offered me a million dollars and the guaranteed privacy of a new identity for the rest of my life to help him with one last simple job. It didn't seem smart to turn him down. Not when it was obvious he could find me whenever he wanted."

"The simple job was to get us," I said.

"Yup, again. He told me who you were and gave me descriptions and some clothes he promised would fit. He told me that you would be released from prison because of a hostage taking. He provided me with the neuron rifle, the black box, and the time and location to wait in ambush. He warned me about the tracking device on the swamp boat. And he told me that once I stopped the swamp boat, because of the tracking device, there would be very little time before more soldiers from the prison began pursuit."

Nate paused. "I wasn't really doing it for the money. More to be left alone. He promised me he didn't mean you any harm, and I decided to take his word for it. I think I decided to believe him to make it easier on me. But I was just fooling myself. I mean, why does someone like him want to go to all the trouble to kidnap you guys?"

I could guess. It had something to do with robot control. But that wasn't something I wanted Nate to know.

"So instead of bringing you to him for whatever reasons he had in mind, I'm now promising to keep you away from him. That might answer all your questions. But only lead to more."

"Like how did the general know all of this?" Ashley said. "And what does he want with us?"

"You said he showed up yesterday," I added. "It wasn't until today that my dad got us out."

Ashley nodded. "Tyce, it was only a half hour before you got out of your cell that I was called down and released. How could anyone have known a full day earlier all of this was going to happen?"

I still didn't even know who my dad had taken hostage and how he'd managed to do it. I wished I hadn't ruined Dad's note by falling in the water.

"Tyce?" Ashley prompted me.

I sure wasn't going to let Nate know what Ashley and I needed to do. Dad had stressed the importance of keeping it secret. Even though Nate was now helping us, it still didn't seem smart to trust him. Not until I knew how much of what he told us was the truth.

I found my voice. "I guess when we know who sent the general, we'll have all the answers."

"Not *all* the answers," Nate corrected me. "Because now you owe me some. Who are you two that my commander wants you so badly? What's with the stuff in the boat? Those robot contraptions? And why were you taken to this high-secrecy Combat Force prison in the Everglades?"

"Ashley," I said, "Dad told me we had some money cards. Did you imprint them?"

"Yes. At least mine. Yours was already imprinted. I think they used a thumbprint from a cup you had handled in prison."

That was good. Although I'd never used a money card on Mars, I knew how they worked. There was a special holo-gram place on the card that would hold only one thumbprint. Computers at banks, money machines, or store cash registers compared the thumbprint of the card with the thumbprint of the person with the card. If both prints matched, the transac-tion went through. If they didn't match, the reading machine immediately destroyed the card. This meant Ashley and I were safe from Nate. He couldn't just take our money cards and get rid of us. He needed Ashley and me to get the money.

"You're not answering my questions," Nate said firmly.

"I'd like to trade you something else instead," I answered. After all, Dad had said we had unlimited use of the money cards.

"What's that?"

As the darkness fell upon us, I gave Nate my best smile

as I made my offer. "How much money will it take for you to help us get where we need to go?"

"Where would that be?"

I coughed. "Ashley?"

She gave Nate a weak grin. "We, uh, can't tell you. Yet."

CHAPTER 12

Nate stared at the campfire. Ashley had fallen asleep in her sleeping bag. I sat to the side in my wheelchair.

I couldn't sleep. My arm itched, and there was a big lump on the surface of my skin. Nate told me it must be from the mosquito bite. I told him the mosquito had bitten me higher on my arm than that. When he laughed at me, I didn't bother going into detail about how that old man in the prison had jabbed my arm.

I watched the fire flicker beyond my toes. Nate had made sure to keep the fire as small as possible so it couldn't be spotted by military pursuers. Suddenly, surrounded by the hum of mosquitoes, I felt lonely and afraid. It was a different kind of fear than I'd felt when all those crises had happened under the dome on Mars—the oxygen leak, the hostile takeover of the dome, and when Dad, Director Rawling, and I had almost been blown up by a black box under our platform buggy. I'd been on Mars—a world I knew well—then. Now I was on Earth, an alien place for me. Dad was in a military prison. And Mom and Rawling, the only other two adults I could count on, were 50 million miles away.

Yet now there was so much for Ashley and me to do. She'd spent most of her life in something she called the Institute, where she'd received her robot training along with 23 other kids her age. She'd only been able to tell Dad and me a few things about it during the trip from Mars to Earth, and we had intended to wait for a secure Internet link to try to use those clues. But would that be enough for us to find it?

I wanted to start keyboarding my thoughts.

Starting tomorrow, we have only five days left of our countdown. If we find out where the Institute is, will that be enough time to reach it?

Even if we find the place in time, what then? How can we get in, if it's surrounded by guards? How exactly are we supposed to go about exposing it to the world through the media?

And what if we can't trust Nate? What will happen to Dad if we fail?

On Mars, I'd learned the habit of keeping a journal. I'd found it helped me sort my thoughts. I had the comp-board with me, and it was tempting to add to my journal now. Especially because I could analyze all the angles once they were written down. But I didn't want Nate to be tempted to take the comp-board from me and read the journal to learn more about Ashley and me. He already knew we were worth big bucks if he delivered us to his former commander. If he found out how much more we were worth as experimental technology, he might decide to change his mind about helping us.

Without a way to get my thoughts down in my journal, it felt like my head was filled with rolling marbles.

I sighed and looked up at the stars. They didn't look as clear from Earth as from Mars. Logically I knew why, of course. Earth's atmosphere distorted the light waves. But logic didn't take away my sense of awe at the beauty of the stars as they seemed to twinkle.

I thought of all I had seen on my first day on Earth outside the prison. How incredible it was to see everything that lived out in the open. On Mars, nothing lived outside the dome. Without that little man-made bubble of air and moisture for protection, life couldn't exist. But here on Earth . . .

"Kid?" Nate said, appearing concerned. "You all right?"

"Sure," I said, hiding my worries.

"You want to tell me about all this gear you have? Those things look like robots and . . ."

"Robots?" I forced myself to laugh. "You don't see any equipment to run them, do you?"

It made me glad I hadn't made him curious about

any information in my comp-board. Before Nate could say anything else, a loud, groaning roar echoed from out of the darkness.

"Relax," Nate said. The fire's tiny glow must have been enough light for him to see me flinch. "Male gator. Letting the world know he's here."

"Oh."

"He'll mind his own business," said Nate. "We're fine here."

"Oh."

"You're interesting to watch." Nate chuckled. "You look around as if the world is one giant candy store. And I agree. It's unbelievably amazing. But because most people see it every day, they take it for granted. Living in the swamp, I had to learn all over again how incredible the process of life and ecology is."

I almost blurted out that I had never seen it before. Even so, it seemed difficult to think that people would take all of this for granted.

I nodded. I, too, had come to understand that there's more to life than what a person can see or hear or touch.

I wanted to be able to trust Nate completely. But Dad had said to trust no one. I finally asked one of the questions that had been bugging me. "Why did you decide to live alone in the swamp?"

"Tell you what," Nate said, grinning, "I'll tell you where I came from if you tell me where you came from."

"Can't," I said after a few seconds.

"Wish you could," he said, "but you're old enough to decide who you can trust."

The alligator in the nearby swamp roared again. A few minutes of silence passed.

"Good night, kid from nowhere," Wild Man finally said.

I did feel like a kid from nowhere. Like an alien on Earth. In a wheelchair, when most people could walk. With a spinal plug that made me even more of a freak. I knew Nate had been joking, but it still hit too close to the truth. I didn't answer him.

He must have felt my coldness in the silence between us, but he spoke kindly. "You already told me you don't need help getting into your sleeping bag. So I'll wake you in plenty of time tomorrow morning."

He crawled into his own sleeping bag.

And left me alone in my wheelchair, staring at the fire, feeling very alone.

CHAPTER 13

The smell of the fire woke me up just before dawn. Along with another interesting smell.

"Eat quickly," Nate said from where he was crouched beside the fire on our miniature island in the middle of the Everglades. "We've got about two hours to reach our meeting point."

I was still in my sleeping bag. The night before Nate had given me a pair of blue pants. He called them jeans. I also wore a T-shirt and a sweater.

I let Nate help me out of the sleeping bag into my wheelchair, impressed all over again at how powerful he was.

Nate went back to the fire, then handed me a green bowl filled with brown liquid. I wasn't familiar with the smooth hard material. *Plastic?*

He grinned at the puzzlement on my face. "Turtle soup. Remember? Slurp it right from the shell."

I nodded and took a taste. A strange texture and rather drippy. But not bad. Nate's version of Earth food was much better than the nute tubes on Mars.

Nate noticed Ashley had awakened as well. He handed her a bowl. She ate it from her sleeping bag.

"Hmmm," she said, after a slurp.

"Finish it quick and get ready to go," he told her. "The sooner we leave, the sooner we arrive."

"Where?" I asked. The sky was getting brighter, and I shivered in my sleeping bag in the predawn cold. Already the sounds of birds filled the air. As if they were happy to be alive. I couldn't blame them. Earth was fascinating.

"It's no coincidence that I chose this route away from the base," Nate put in. "It was the direction that put us closest to the interstate. I've got a friend who handles a mag-strip truck on the north-south route. He usually brings me supplies once every two weeks, and I meet him at a truck stop on the highway on the outer limits of the Everglades. After my ex-commander showed up the other day, I called this friend and set up a meeting with him for today. Just in case I needed to get away from this area quickly."

No coincidence? It seemed like too much of a coincidence. I was immediately suspicious. "How did you know you'd need him?"

Nate smiled grimly. "When I was running operations, I always set up a fallback plan in case anything went wrong. The way it looks now, not only is my ex-commander going to be looking for me after not showing up with you two, but so are the Combat Force people we escaped yesterday. To me, this definitely qualifies as something going wrong."

A little under two hours later, Nate let the swamp boat glide to a stop at the edge of some trees.

As the motor died, I heard a strange whooshing rumble on the other side of the trees. The thick green underbrush did not let me see more than 10 feet ahead, so I couldn't tell what was making the noise.

"He'll have parked his trailer as close to the path as possible," Nate said as he jumped from the boat and tied the rope to a tree. "That's how he does it when he delivers my supplies. So I'll make a couple of trips. I'll bring up our equipment first, then come back for you guys."

"Um, sure," I said. We didn't have much choice except to trust him. The alternative was to try to move by ourselves, which would be next to impossible. For two reasons. One, I was in my wheelchair, which could not roll through swampland. And two, Ashley and I didn't really know where we were going. Yet.

Nate jumped back on the swamp boat and rolled each

robot forward. He jumped off the boat and reached up for the upper body of the first titanium robot. He tilted it forward across his shoulder.

"At least these things are light enough to carry. But they're going to be a pain to travel with," he said. "I have a feeling they're the reason I was offered so much money for you. Sure you don't want to tell me about them?"

I shook my head. As did Ashley.

"Remember," I said. Ashley and I had talked with him earlier about our money cards and the unlimited funds. We weren't in danger that he'd steal them from us, because he didn't have the identity prints to use them. "When you get us where we need to go, you will get your million."

He grinned. "I remember. Of course, you still haven't told me where you need to go."

We didn't know yet. But this wasn't something I wanted to tell him.

With the robot over his shoulder, Nate turned and disappeared up the path. Thirty seconds later he reappeared and did the same with the second robot. He came back for a duffel bag with his own supplies. Then for me and Ashley.

To get me off the boat, he first lifted me and then set me on the ground. Next he went back for my wheelchair before setting me in it and rolling me forward on the path toward the rumbling noises.

Ashley followed, carrying our gear.

When we reached the end of the path, one row of trees screened us from what lay beyond. Both robots and Nate's duffel bag sat nearby.

Finally I saw the source of the rumbling noise.

"Trucks!" I said in triumph, recognizing them from the DVD-gigaroms. There was a parking lot filled with huge trucks and trailers. And on the other side was a highway, with vehicles rumbling down the pavement at high speeds. I never would have guessed they'd be so big.

"You sound like you've never seen a truck before." Nate again eyeballed me.

I didn't answer.

Ahead of us, a truck had backed up to the edge of the parking lot. The back trailer doors were open. That, I guessed, was our destination. A truck stop. As Nate had explained, it was a rest area off the interstate where trucks fueled.

There were probably 50 trucks, so I wasn't too worried that we would be noticed. Until I saw the Combat Force soldiers guarding trucks with Federation colors. Would they see us as we loaded our stuff onto the truck?

Before I could say anything to Ashley, there was a loud explosion.

And the front end of one of the military trucks blossomed with smoke.

CHAPTER 14

"Hurry! Hurry! Hurry!" Nate urged Ashley. "As soon as they figure out it's only a smoke bomb, they'll start wondering why. And we need to be gone by then."

Ashley ran toward the back door of the trailer, carrying what she could.

Nate helped her up.

He ran back for the robots. One by one he lifted them into the trailer. He threw her his duffel bag. That left only me in the wheelchair.

Nate rolled me forward. With a loud grunt he picked both me and the wheelchair up and hoisted me into the trailer. Then he hopped in and swung both doors, putting us into temporary darkness.

"I think we're safe." His voice echoed in the trailer.

A lurch told us the truck was moving forward.

I held my breath. If any of the soldiers were going to stop the truck, it would be in the next minute as it left this parking area.

I heard rumbling as the truck gained speed.

And finally, when I could hold my breath no longer, I relaxed.

We were on the highway.

Light hit us from the front of the trailer as a door opened.

It revealed stacks of heavy crates between the front and us. The outline of a man showed in the light. The man walked toward us on a small catwalk that led from the cab to the trailer. Nate had told us earlier that these newer trucks included sleeping quarters in the trailer.

"Not even close, Nate," came his deep voice. "No hitches. Just like the old days. Nothing like a good old smoke bomb to distract the enemy, huh?"

"Whistler was one of the best bomb guys I had," Nate said quietly. "We called him Whistler because he whistled all the time but couldn't carry a tune in a bucket. Still, I'd trust him with my life."

Whistler reached us. Nate shook his hand. In the dimness I could barely see his face, but I could tell he was African-American.

"Ashley and Tyce," Nate said proudly, "this is Whistler."

Whistler's white teeth showed in a wide grin as he shook both our hands. "Ee-yew. You guys don't smell that pretty, let me tell you. How long you been in the swamps?"

"Too long," Nate said with a laugh.

"Is there another driver?" I asked.

"No," Whistler answered. "Should there be?"

"You're back here and . . ." I'd never been in a truck before, but even I knew that someone should be at the steering wheel.

"Mag-strips," Whistler said.

"Mag-strips?"

"You from another planet, kid?" Whistler joked.

Here we go again, I thought.

"Everyone knows how mag-strips work," Whistler continued.

"Go easy on him, Whistler," Nate said quickly. "He asks crazy questions, but I know he's not stupid." Then he turned to me. "All the interstate highways have mag-strips embedded every five feet in the pavement. They read computer sensors in the truck's axles. Between GPS and the main computer at the trucking company's head office, the trucks are guided at the right speed the right distance apart."

"This truck can be tracked anywhere it goes?"

"Tracked and guided. But only on the interstate highways. The drivers are needed for when the trucks have to exit and head into the cities."

"Yeah," Whistler announced, "it's a great job for long-haul drivers. Once we get our rigs from the city streets or the truck stops onto the highway, we can kick back and relax."

He jerked his thumb toward the rear of our trailer. "Except for the Combat Force drivers we left back at the truck stop. They're under such tight computer supervision, they can't even blink without some commander knowing it. Which is a waste, considering they always travel in a pack of 10 trucks. What's one of the drivers going to do? Peel off and try to drive away from the escort trucks? Not even a payload of tantalum is worth that kind of risk."

"Tantalum?" I echoed.

"This kid is from Mars, isn't he?" Whistler joked to Nate. "Tantalum. The miracle metal they've been mining from the moon. Those trucks you saw back there? All of them came from the Everglades space base. That's where the shuttles land with tantalum from the Earth-Moon orbits." He paused. "Where exactly are you guys from? All Nate told me was he needed to get you out of this area."

"More important than where they're from," Nate interrupted, "is for me to know where they're going. Which is something they refused to tell me until we made it out of the Everglades. Now would be as good a time as any, Tyce."

"Not so fast," I said. "When can we get to the nearest library?"

CHAPTER 15

After about four hours on the interstate, we stopped at a motel just off the road.

Whistler rented a room near the back of the motel and parked his truck in such a way that passersby couldn't see inside the trailer as he opened the back doors. During our time on the highway, Nate had given us a couple of reasons why we should stop, and Ashley and I saw no reason to disagree.

Especially for reason number one.

Showers! After a couple of days in prison and our time in the Everglades, we needed it.

Nate carried me into the room. Ashley followed. She went into the bathroom first while Nate and I waited in the outer room and watched television. Then my turn.

I loved it. Whistler had made sure to rent a room that would accommodate my needs from a wheelchair. It was the first shower I'd ever been able to take without worrying how much water I was using. On Mars, water was far too scarce, so we were allowed showers only twice a month. The rest of the time we used an evaporating gel as soap.

Here, under the hot water that streamed down like it would never end, I couldn't believe that people on Earth had a luxury like this any day they wanted. I finally finished when I heard banging on the bathroom door.

Then Nate's turn. He went in with his duffel bag while Ashley and I flipped channels. We'd never actually used a television before—she because of her time in the Institute and I because of my time on Mars. I was familiar with a lot of the programs, though, from the DVD-gigaroms I'd watched on Mars.

The television hung from the ceiling, so Ashley and I could each lie on a bed and watch.

After I flipped through all the channels twice, Nate stepped out of the bathroom. But he didn't look like Nate.

"Wow!" Ashley said.

"Is that you?" I asked.

Nate had given himself a haircut and shaved his beard. Plus, he'd changed from his crusty wilderness clothing into a black turtleneck and tan pants. I almost didn't recognize him.

"Yes, it's me," Nate said. "We're on the run. Last thing I want is to draw attention to us by looking like a hermit."

I kept flipping channels as he spoke.

"Whistler's not back yet?" he asked.

The truck was still outside, but Nate had asked Whistler to take a taxi to a car rental place to rent a van.

"He—" Ashley stopped as a car horn beeped outside. She smiled. "He's right here."

"Good," Nate said. "I'll say good-bye to him for all of us. You guys wait here while I unload the stuff from the trailer to the van. Then the three of us can travel by ourselves."

"Hang on!" I shouted. It felt like my eyes were bugging out of my head as I pointed at the television.

"Yes?" Nate looked confused. Filling the screen was the face of an old man handling a press conference.

"It's him!"

"Sure it's him. It's big news, this week's annual gathering of the Governors of Justice. In New York."

"You have television in your cabin in the Everglades?" Ashley asked.

"No. Radio."

"Oh," she said.

"You don't get it," I told them. This wasn't the time for idle conversation. "It's him!"

"What's the big deal?" Nate put in. "Everybody knows who he is. The supreme governor. Head of the Governors of Justice. Aside from the president of the World United Federation, he's the most powerful man in the world."

"But it's him!" I claimed excitedly. "The guy my dad held hostage in the Combat Force prison!"

CHAPTER 16

A half hour later we were on the interstate again, where GPS and an onboard computer system in the van guided us among the other vehicles through the mag-strip sensors embedded in the pavement.

I looked around. All I saw were large trucks, cars, and vans traveling at precisely the same speed we were, since the computer system maintained the proper distance between each vehicle.

Trees and hanging vines formed walls of green on both sides of the interstate. Over the previous hours of travel, the highway had lost some of its flatness and straightness. Nate had promised that as we traveled farther north, the surroundings would change even more.

"Do you like your library?" Nate asked, turning from

behind the steering wheel to Ashley and me in the back of the van.

"Library?" I asked.

"Sure."

I was so used to Nate with a beard, it was strange to see his smile surrounded by smooth skin. "I know you're carrying a comp-board. We'll just plug it in to the Internet as we drive. You can find anything you need."

I sure hoped he was right.

"You know we have a comp-board?" Ashley repeated.

"Of course. Think I'd take you guys anywhere without searching all of your possessions while you slept? I was disappointed I needed a password to access the information."

It made me glad I hadn't gone into my journal earlier.

"That's not fair," Ashley said.

"Who said I had to be fair? We've got two different branches of military after us. My ex-commander and your prison people. But you won't tell me why. You want me to take you somewhere, but you won't give me the location. You won't even tell me why you were held in prison or what those robots are for. Plus, I've been offered a lot of money for you. By Cannon. And by you guys. Which leads me to another thing. How you have that much money. Face it. There's a lot of questions about all of this. I'd be dumb not to find out what I can."

"I still don't think it's fair." Ashley frowned.

Nate gave her a charming grin. "As long as you don't kick me in the shins again."

"Guys?" I interrupted. "Library?"

"One wireless Internet connection is up front here," Nate said, still grinning as Ashley kept giving him a dirty look. "And there's another in the back beside your wheelchair."

"We'll take the one in the back where you can't watch," I said, returning the same kind of grin he gave us. "We'd hate for you to find out anything else until we were ready."

The hum of the pavement beneath the van's wheels would screen our conversation from Nate. "Okay," I whispered to Ashley. "I know we spent hours and hours talking about this on the spaceship, but I want to be sure I've got it right. When they took you from the Institue, All you saw was 'Arker,' right?"

"It was night," she said, sitting directly beside my wheelchair. "Remember, they had me drugged with something when they took me out of there. I could barely keep even one eye open. It was like a real bad fever, where you're not sure if what you are seeing is real or not. We got on a highway, and there was this skinny green sign. I think it said Arker 11."

"Eleven miles to a town or city called Arker." That's what Dad had guessed during our discussions on the Moon Racer. "And you said red mountains, almost like Mars."

"Yes." Her voice was quiet as she remembered.

In a way, her childhood had not been much different

from mine. She'd been raised in the Institute, trapped in a canyon, never seeing anything of the rest of the world. I, of course, had seen just as little of Earth.

We had done a map search on board, using the *Moon Racer*'s computer and one of the library's encyclopedia DVD-gigaroms. Dad had guessed red mountains to be somewhere in the southwestern states. But there was no Arker in Arizona, California, Colorado, Nevada, New Mexico, or Utah.

We weren't, however, without hope. Dad had wanted to do an Internet search as soon as we reached Earth. Of casinos.

"Slipper, Slipper, here we come," I said to Ashley.

"It could have been my imagination," she warned. "I mean, I was drugged and fading quickly. And there it was, a giant red slipper in the sky. To me, it was named Casi. The last thing I saw before I woke up on a space shuttle, headed for Mars."

Unlike Dad, Ashley and I would never have guessed that *Casi* might be the first four letters of the word *Casino*. Or that the giant red slipper in the sky might be a neon sign. Not with our limited experience of Earth things.

I entered the words *slipper* and *casino* into the search directory. Seconds later my screen began to fill with results.

"Here it is," I said, scanning my computer screen. "Lucky Slipper. Red Slipper. Another Lucky Slipper. Another. And another."

I sighed as the search results finished. "There must be

100 results here. Casinos in Arizona, California, Colorado, Nevada, New Jersey, Montana." My Earth geography was limited to what I had memorized as part of my school lessons, but even I knew that all the states I was seeing were hundreds and thousands of miles apart. We had only four more days after today. How could we reach them all on the vague hope that Ashley would recognize something familiar?

"Hey," she exclaimed. "Look!"

I looked above her pointing finger. Near the top of the list. *Red Slipper Casino, Parker, Arizona.*

"Parker?" I whispered. "Not Arker?"

"They've got a link to their own Web site. Take a look."

I clicked. Waiting for the visual seemed to take forever. Slowly a photo of a giant red slipper glowing in the night filled the screen.

"Scary." She shivered. "It's bringing all the bad memories of that night back to me again."

"Ashley!" It was my turn to point. Brochure information lined the bottom of the screen.

Located on the Colorado River, the Red Slipper Casino is a favorite stopping place for vacationers who visit nearby Lake Havasu. The reddish mountains nearby serve as a beautiful backdrop to a place of warm hospitality. . . .

"Reddish mountains!" she said, evidently seeing what I saw.

"Nate!" I shouted. "How far is it to Arizona from here?"

"Three days by highway," he answered. "But I have to tell you, I never intended on taking this van much farther than it will go on a tank of gas."

Without his help, we had no chance. How else could we transport two robots and someone in a wheelchair across the country? Especially with so few days left?

"Is it because we haven't given you any money yet?" I asked, ready to beg. "If you need to go to a bank—"

"Relax," he called back to me. "I have no intention of seeing either of you use your money cards."

Fear sickened my stomach.

Wild Man continued to speak to us from the front. "Don't you think they would use the computer record of where you spent or withdrew money to track your progress and find you?"

He didn't give us the chance to answer his question. "So I'm going to have to dip into my own accounts until all of this settles."

"Won't they be able to track you by your money trail?" I asked.

"Not a chance," Nate said firmly. "When I went into hiding, I set up fingerprint identities on three secret accounts. They might have been able to find me in the swamps but not my money. That's a good thing. Because let me tell you, the next part of our trip might cost a big chunk of money."

CHAPTER 17

"How does $50,000 sound?" Nate asked the woman standing beside him.

Ashley and I remained in the van, peeking and listening through an open window.

"Sounds like too much," came a gravelly voice. The woman looked a little younger than my mom, and her name was Red. I easily understood why. Her deep red hair glinted like fire in the afternoon sun. Freckles covered all of her exposed skin, including neck, face, and strong-looking forearms that stuck out from her rolled-up blue sleeves.

"I want you to get $50,000 because we're old friends," Nate bargained. "You're telling me you want less?"

"No, I'm telling you I want more."

"Let me get this straight. I offer $50,000. You say it sounds like too much. But you want more."

Behind us came the roar of an airplane engine. I twisted my head to peer out the other window of the van. Heat waves shimmered off a long, black runway cut into the trees. A small, single-jet airplane approached, twisting slightly as it angled to land, the air whooshing through the turbines in the plane's nose.

We had made it into the northern half of Florida, to this small private airport. Nearby hangars held parked airplanes. Other than the runway and the hangars, the airport had a small trailer used as an office. That's where we had parked. Nate had gone in to talk to Red, and they'd stepped out here into the sunshine a few minutes later.

"Sure, I want more," Red answered Nate's question. "That's if I even rented it to you. You've got two kids in a rented van, and once you get in the air I have no way of knowing where you're headed or when you'll be back. And you offer me triple what I would expect for a couple days' use of an airplane. That makes me worried."

"So worried that you won't trust a man who spent seven years with you in the same platoon?" Nate asked quietly.

"I owe you my life," Red said. "I haven't forgotten that. Which is why I'm not going to make a call to the Combat Force goons who stopped by here yesterday asking about you."

"What!"

"I don't believe what they're saying about you. And I don't want to know the details either. But that's the other reason I'm worried. You're on the run. My guess is that the Combat Force is checking all your old friends, because we're the ones you would turn to. And if you're on the run, I can't rent you one of the airport's planes. Even for more than $50,000."

"You know I can fly anything," Nate argued, "and you'll get the airplane back. If anything happens to it, I'll cover the cost of the damage. You have my word on it."

"Your word is as good as gold," Red agreed. "Everyone in the platoon knew that. But I still can't rent you an airplane. If the Combat Force comes back and checks my records, they'll know two things. That I didn't call back when you showed up. And that I helped you escape. After the way they threatened me yesterday . . . I mean, with my husband dead, I can't do much for my kids if I spend time in jail."

"Yeah." Nate sighed. "I heard about your husband and the car accident. I was real sorry for you. I understand. I can't put you in that kind of position. I appreciate you sticking your neck out to tell me they're on the lookout for us."

Red shrugged. "Not a big deal. You remember Skids? The skinny guy in the platoon who was lousy with directions?"

"Yeah."

"He runs a car dealership on the other side of the state. Who would have guessed, huh? Makes millions, and I remember he needed help tying his laces."

Nate laughed. "Who would have guessed?"

"Anyway," Red continued, "he called me yesterday. Said the Combat Force had dropped in on him, too."

"Not good."

"Here's what's really strange," Red added. "Remember Cannon?"

"No one forgets a platoon commander, Red. He's a general now. One of the highest-ranking generals in the Combat Force."

"Yeah," Red returned. "Get this. Cannon showed up *after* the other Combat Force soldiers came around with questions. Alone. It was like he wasn't working with his own people. Skids told me the same thing, that Cannon showed up after the others. Now does that make sense to you?"

"Not much makes sense to me anymore," Nate answered.

"Tell you what," Red continued. "I'm going to give Skids a call. He owes you a favor too. I'll ask him to tell the Combat Force you stopped by there trying to buy a car from him cheap. They'll swarm that side of the state looking for you. You'll have a lot easier time escaping in the other direction. It's the least we can do for you."

How much good will that really do us to escape the Combat Force but still be in the van? I wondered. As Nate had told us earlier, the only chance of getting to Arizona on time was by airplane. But this was the only place Nate had a chance of getting one. And now it looked like that chance was cut off. We needed the airplane or else . . .

I thought of Dad waiting in the prison cell. I thought of the countdown of passing days. I felt a sharp pain in my palms and saw that I was clenching my fists so hard in frustration that my nails cut into my skin.

"See ya, Red," Nate said.

"See ya, Nate."

Nate began to open the driver's-side door of the van, but Red's next words stopped him.

"Be a shame, wouldn't it," Red told Nate, her back to him, "if someone knew that the hangar at the end of the runway had a twin Otter with the door unlocked and the keys in it. It's an old beater hanging around, a relic from the old days, but it still runs really well."

Red turned toward Nate and grinned. "Be even more of a shame if someone knew that twin Otter airplane was fueled and ready to go, like it had been parked there for someone to take on short notice ever since those Combat Force goons showed up and threatened me not to help you. Biggest shame of all is that I might not even notice the twin Otter was gone for a few days, and by the time I filed the paperwork on it, who knows, that someone might even have returned it."

"Real shame," Nate agreed. He smiled.

Red reached out and shook Nate's hand. "Thanks for trusting me enough to come here. I still owe you plenty."

I wasn't sure if I understood what I'd just heard.

"Got to be going," Red finished. "My favorite show just

started. Inside the trailer, I have to crank the volume on my television to hear it above my air conditioner. When I'm in there watching, it's so loud, planes can come and go and I don't have any idea of what's happening out on the runway."

Nate got into the van. He started the engine.

"By the way," Red told him through the open window, "there's a little trail behind that hangar that leads into the trees. I suspect if anyone ever drove a couple hundred yards down that trail with a rented van, it would be weeks before anyone noticed where it was parked."

"Thanks," Nate said.

"Thanks for what?" Red grinned again. "I have no idea what you're talking about. Right? Not a thing."

CHAPTER 18

What an incredible world!

We flew in the twin Otter at 2,500 feet, low enough to see the changing terrain. As the hours passed in the airplane and as I traced our westward path on a map, Nate pointed out different landmarks. The three of us were equipped with headsets that let us speak and hear easily above the roar of the twin prop engines.

Less than 20 minutes after takeoff, we'd reached the Gulf of Mexico. With the beauty of the clouds and sun and the endless stretch of light bouncing off the whitecaps of the waves below, I'd hardly been able to breathe.

Then we'd cut back over land, crossing Alabama. Everywhere I looked, it was green. I was staggered to think of all the life that swarmed the earth and the sky and the water. Later, after refueling, we had crossed the Mississippi. I'd been unable to comprehend a flow of water hundreds upon hundreds upon hundreds of miles long, all of it filled with fish and insects and frogs and turtles.

Then the landscape had slowly changed, as the carpet of green trees began to break into open areas and we began to cross the Great Plains. Nate told us that less than 200 years earlier, millions of buffalo had lived there, and I tried to imagine the immense herds in a sea of waving grass.

We had to stop after the first day of flying, because Nate didn't want to fly at night in the mountains. I didn't understand why he wanted to be cautious until we began to fly again the next morning.

At first, the mountains were just blue smudges across the horizon ahead of us. Then the snowcapped peaks came into focus. And then we were in them, with Nate following highways below us so we could make it through the passes. Wind shook us from side to side until our wingtips seemed to brush the snow and the granite. It was strange to imagine our plane as just a little speck floating high above the pine forests and rivers.

Time and again on our journey I stared—and wondered what it would have been like to grow up on Earth and to be able to see this incredible world every single day.

As we reached the other side of the mountains, moving into the western half of New Mexico and finally into Arizona, the red rocks and brown valleys reminded me in a small way of Mars.

When I thought of Mars, I thought about Mom. I wondered if she knew somehow that Dad was in trouble.

And I thought about Dad.

Especially of the fact that, including today, there were only four days left of our countdown.

"There's the Parker Dam!" Nate pointed out the window to our left. "And downriver, the town of Parker."

He banked the airplane as I checked the map. To our right, a long, narrow lake bounced brilliant blue light from the reds and browns of the desert. This was Lake Havasu, formed by the Parker Dam. On the other side of the dam, the Colorado River was a snake of blue winding through more desert reds and browns. From the air, the town of Parker appeared to be a neatly laid grid of miniature houses.

"Anything look familiar yet?" Nate asked Ashley.

When we had stopped last night, Ashley and I had agreed that we at least had to trust Nate enough to fill him in on a few details. Then he might be able to help us pinpoint our search. And so we had.

Ashley shook her head. She hadn't spoken much over

the last few hours. I wondered if she was afraid to return to the place where she had spent most of her life. Now it would seem like a prison to her. But then—among the others who, like her, had been in the Institute as long as they could remember—she didn't know any other kind of life. Then her life had seemed normal.

"I'll take us in a few circles," Nate said. "I know things look different in the air than from the ground, but you never know."

All Ashley had been able to tell us last night was that the children could see a strange tall mountain peak from the open area where they were allowed to play. She said all the kids had called it the Unsleeping Soldier because it looked like it guarded them.

Twenty minutes later we were still circling. The red mountains threw dark shadows into deep canyons.

"I'm going to have to take us down," Nate announced into our headsets. "We'll find a place to stay for the night. Tomorrow we'll drive around in a rented vehicle and keep looking."

Tomorrow. One more day closer to the deadline.

"Hang on!" Ashley shouted. "There!"

Sure enough, one of the peaks did look like a tall, skinny man.

"There?" Nate repeated.

"There!" Ashley insisted.

"Check it out, Tyce." Nate motioned toward the map.

I studied the map briefly, then circled a place with my pencil. "Makes sense. Abandoned military base," I said, reading the map. "No trespassing."

"Exactly. I think we've found it," Nate said enthusiastically. "First thing tomorrow, we'll check it out."

Which would have been a great plan.

Except as we were watching TV in our motel room late that evening, there was a sharp crack of breaking glass.

I caught a glimpse of a small ball as it tumbled across the floor.

Nate dived for it, but it was too late.

The flash of light and the boom of the explosion came at the same time.

And when the bitter smoke hit my face, I gagged once, then sank into blackness.

CHAPTER 19

I woke up in my wheelchair with a dry mouth and a slight headache.

A breeze came in through the broken window. It was still dark outside, and the clock in the motel room read 3:15 a.m. The TV was still on, with the volume turned down. Its dim glow showed that Nate had been duct-taped to one chair. He was blinking himself awake too. Ashley lay on the floor, where she had fallen out of her chair in front of the TV. She was still unconscious.

A large man in army fatigues stood against the door. Shaved bald, he had a square face with a bent nose. The neuron gun in his right hand was pointed at Nate. "You're getting soft and old. I really expected you to be somewhere in the desert, in a camp guarded by trip lines. This is the price you pay for wanting a place with beds and showers. The Wild Man I remembered from the platoon never would have made the mistake of bunking down where he could be so easily trapped."

The man continued to speak as he shrugged. "But then, the Wild Man I knew never would have turned traitor. Who paid you and how much?"

"Why would I need to be paid to keep you from getting your hands on these kids?" Nate answered in a level voice. "It's obvious now that *you're* the one who means them harm."

"Me?"

"Give me a break, Cannon. These kids have robots. And they're on the run from a Combat Force base and prison. That alone tells me they have something so valuable that they need help. Somehow I don't think you represent official channels here. Otherwise there would be Combat Force soldiers with you and we'd already be outside and loaded into a military truck. You wouldn't have come to me in the Everglades with your little plan to steal them as they escaped from that prison either."

Nate paused.

"Ashley, Tyce, pardon my manners for beginning a conversation without letting you know who this is," Nate said, spreading his arms wide, making a mockery of his elaborate introduction of the man with the neuron gun. "General Jeb McNamee. Known as Cannon, because when we were friends—*when* we were friends—I liked to call him a big shot. But I guess our friendship is now over, because I refuse to like anyone who would mean you two any harm."

So this was Cannon, the general who had first approached Nate and given him the equipment and timetable to capture us from the swamp boat.

"*Me* mean them harm? I'm trying to *rescue* them from the Combat Force," Cannon snapped. "Something that would have been a lot easier if you hadn't run with them. So let me ask you again. Who paid you? The Terratakers? Because if I find out you had anything to do with my son being taken away from me—"

"General, somewhere you've been out in the sun too long without a hat."

Without warning, the general pulled the trigger of his neuron gun.

I saw and heard nothing. Neuron guns don't make noise. But Nate tilted in his chair and groaned slightly as he fell back into unconsciousness. The neuron blast would have paralyzed half his muscles. I doubted he'd wake for a while.

"You okay?" Cannon asked me.

"Yes, but—"

"Hang on." He stepped past me and returned from the motel bathroom with a glass of water. In my thirst I reached for it, but he was already past me again. He knelt beside

Ashley, who was struggling to sit up. He put his arm behind her back and helped her stand. "Sorry about the punch of that sleeping gas, but I couldn't see any other way to neutralize Nate without putting you both in danger."

Ashley gulped back the water.

"I trust you're here because it's close to the Institute?" Cannon asked. "I mean, when Nate stopped to refuel the airplane yesterday, he didn't go to the trouble of buying a van like he did here."

Like I was going to answer this man?

"I wouldn't mind some water myself," I said from the wheelchair. I had a plan. Not much of one. But the best I could think of.

The general walked into the bathroom again. I rolled forward to block the doorway and turned my head back to Ashley.

"Run!" I whispered to Ashley. "Get the motel manager to call for help!"

Ashley was groggy as she got to her feet. She took a step to the door as Cannon came out of the bathroom with a full glass of water.

"Hey!" he said from behind my wheelchair as she reached the door. He dropped the water and tried pushing my wheelchair out of his way.

I grabbed his belt. "Go!" I shouted at Ashley. "Go!"

She struggled to unbolt the door.

The general swept my hand and wheelchair aside and dived forward. He yanked her away from the door.

"Are you guys crazy?" he said, gently pushing her back toward the center of the room. "Why are you trying to escape when I finally managed to rescue you?"

"Rescue us? You sent Nate to kidnap us," I pointed out. "He's helping us run away from you."

"What?"

"I doubt you have good intentions. There's no way you should have known when and where we were leaving the prison," I continued. "You must be working with Dr. Jordan."

"Now you're telling me you don't even trust your own father." When this man with the huge ugly face frowned, it was not a sight that would help little children sleep better.

"Of course we trust him." Ashley put her hands on her hips in her trademark pose. It was clear she wasn't scared by the general in his army fatigues.

"Then why run with Nate?" Cannon said. "You know that your father and the supreme governor set this up."

Silence.

The general studied my face. Then Ashley's. "I said," he repeated, "you know that your father and the supreme governor set this up. Including the tracking device in your arm. And the money cards that would let us watch your progress if anything went wrong. It was in your father's letter. It had instructions telling you that it was safe for Nate to deliver both of you to me. And I was to help you keep out of the hands of the Combat Force as we found the Institute."

The letter.

"Nice try," I said sarcastically. My dad's cell *had* been wired. The Combat Force knew Dad had given me a letter. This man could easily be making this up.

"Nice try? Now I need to convince you that your father . . ." Cannon shook his head. "Kid, how else would I have known when you would be released? The supreme governor set all this up. Including insisting on visiting your father personally in his cell. That way he could quickly explain to your father what he needed to do, through a handwritten note that couldn't be picked up on the audio, and then get your father's help. The supreme governor allowed himself to be taken as your dad's hostage, securing your release from the base."

Is that why Dad had the dull edge of the blade pressed against the old man's throat?

"And while you were in your dad's cell, the supreme governor jabbed a tracking chip into your arm. That allowed me to pick up from there, once you were away from the base and in the boat."

I remembered the old man grabbing my arm and the stabbing pain. I remembered wondering why Dad had pretended to be angry. All of that to plant a tracking chip? My face must have been an open book of confusion.

"Tracking chip. That's how I found you," Cannon explained. "I've been following you guys for two days, just waiting for the right time to move in. Come on. All of it was in the letter. You did read your dad's letter, right?"

Only two people knew I hadn't read that letter. Me. And Ashley, whom I had just told a few hours ago, while Nate was taking a shower and Ashley and I were watching TV.

Besides Ashley, only one person knew the letter had been destroyed by water. Me.

Which meant the general had no reason to bluff me. He really thought I had read the letter. He really thought I knew all the stuff he was telling us.

My words came out as if my tongue were a block of wood. "You mean that you were sent by my dad? And that Nate was sent by you?"

"Stop playing games. I had to send Nate because there are too many Terratakers in the Combat Force. If any of them found out I was behind this mission to rescue you, it was too possible for this information to reach the Terratakers. And with them holding my son hostage, there was too much danger he would die."

He pointed at Nate, disgust on his face. "It was a good plan, until Nate turned traitor and took off with you both. That cost us a lot of time. Now we're down to a few days before all of it happens."

"All of what?"

Now it was Cannon's turn to be confused. "That's part of it. We don't know quite what, just that Jordan has planned something big. And bad. You know that, too, otherwise—"

My face must have looked blank.

"You did read the letter, didn't you?"

"It, um . . . fell into . . . the swamp when we were being chased." I stopped. "No, I didn't read it."

Comprehension smoothed out the concerned wrinkles on the general's face. "No wonder Nate believed he was rescuing you from me. No wonder you have no idea what is waiting for us."

"Waiting for us?" I gave him a weak smile. "Is there any chance you can prove my father sent you?"

He nodded. "It's about time you asked. Does the phrase 'Twinkie Nose' ring a bell?"

I winced. "Yes."

"Twinkie Nose?" Ashley asked. "Isn't a Twinkie a—?"

"Yes, yes," I said quickly. "But that's all I'm telling."

When I was too little to remember, my mom said she'd catch me picking my nose so often it was like I was trying to eat a Twinkie, which she'd explained was an Earth snack. When I was old enough to be embarrassed about this, if I misbehaved in public, she would threaten to call me Twinkie Nose and explain why to everybody listening. That always settled me down.

"So now you know your father sent me, right?" Cannon said.

I nodded. "Do you think you could start from the beginning? With all the stuff in the letter that I didn't get a chance to read?"

CHAPTER 20

A couple of hours later, dawn broke across the hills. The sky was rose colored, with a hint of orange growing brighter as the sun almost broke across the jagged lines of the horizon.

We drove on the main highway in a van that Nate had purchased from a used-car dealer. The small town of Parker and the motel were only a few minutes behind us, but already the desert was totally without any houses or signs or any other marks of human life. There was no other traffic. Because the sand was almost red, it felt like we were on Mars. The weight of gravity, however, and my tiredness told me otherwise.

"Let me get this straight," Nate, now partially recovered from the neuron blast, said. He sat in the passenger seat. "The supreme governor set this up."

Nate had only been awake for a few minutes. We'd left the motel quickly, taking time only to load up the van with all our gear and the robots and pay the bill.

"From the beginning," Cannon said, not taking his eyes off the road as he drove. "We even planned it down to the tracking chip in Tyce's arm. Without that, I'd have never found you."

"Why is the supreme governor involved?" Nate asked, incredulous. "I mean, he's the most powerful government person in the world. What does he—?"

"His grandson is in the Institute. Just like my son," the general replied harshly.

Grandson? Son? I had a dozen questions of my own. But I kept my mouth shut and listened.

"We shouldn't have been arrested when we arrived on Earth," Ashley said. "It was Dr. Jordan who tried to kill us. He's the one who should have been put in prison."

"Some of us know that now," Cannon answered. He didn't turn his head as he drove. His neck seemed like chiseled granite.

"Who is 'us'?" Nate interrupted.

"A group of the top World United Federation Combat Force generals. You see, as the *Moon Racer* approached Earth, the signals sent to the Combat Force informed us that the ship's pilot and some of the crew had turned against two high-level government passengers, including Dr. Jordan. They'd been killed and ejected into space."

That was exactly what Dad had informed me in his note.

"A total lie," I said indignantly. "It was the opposite. Dr. Jordan and Luke Daab had complete control of the ship's computer. They must have secretly changed all of our regular transmissions."

"We know that now, but how could we tell differently at the time? Furthermore, we had no way of knowing that Dr. Jordan was alive and on his way to Earth. Since then, we've confirmed that. Intelligence sources tell us a cargo ship returning from the Moon picked up his escape pod. From there, Dr. Jordan has disappeared."

And now he's somewhere on Earth, planning something we have to stop. Only we don't quite know what.

"What changed?" Nate asked quietly. I could tell his old belief in his platoon commander was back. "How did you find out the truth and decide that the report was false?"

"Two things. The first was Tyce's computer."

My computer?

"Naturally we went through all the confiscated equipment. Including Tyce's computer. A program broke his password code. It had a journal of the *Moon Racer*'s voyage. That gave us a different story of the space trip. We weren't sure whether to believe it, but it cast enough doubt that when prisoner Blaine Steven asked for a private meeting with the supreme governor, we arranged it."

"Blaine Steven . . . ," Nate prompted.

"Former director of the Mars Project. A man with plenty of political clout even though he hadn't been on Earth for over a decade."

Blaine Steven. The man who'd secretly been working for Dr. Jordan all those years he'd been on Mars. And yet, once aboard the *Moon Racer*, Steven had been worried that Dr. Jordan would try to kill him. For good reason.

"Blaine Steven," Cannon continued, "didn't know the details, only that Dr. Jordan intended some kind of Terrataker mission as soon as he got back to Earth. And with the rest of what Blaine Steven told us, things began to make sense. We are now trying our best to stop Jordan, but we're working in the dark. That's why we need Tyce and Ashley so badly. It goes way beyond trying to rescue my own son and the governor's grandson."

Cannon began to slow down. In the growing light of day, I could hardly recognize the upcoming turnoff as a road. It was more like a set of tire tracks leading into the desert hills. He drove off the highway onto the tracks.

"Cannon," Nate said quietly, "where we need to go, this van doesn't have a chance."

"We're not going there in the van. Remember, I do have a few military connections."

"Which is why the supreme governor brought you into this?" Nate asked.

The van bounced and jolted. Dust began to film the windows.

"He brought me into this because he could trust me. As you well know, like most high levels of the Federation government, even the top levels of our Combat Force are infiltrated by Terrataker rebels. Just like Dr. Jordan. With crucial peace talks coming up in New York, the rebels are going out of their way to bring war. If any of the Terratakers found out about Tyce and Ashley and their robot connections, what we're about to do next would have no chance. That's why the supreme governor and I needed to privately arrange Tyce and Ashley's escape. And why I brought you in to help. I wanted you to bring them to me before the Combat Force could track them down again. We figured with Tyce and Ashley's help, we also might find the secret location of the Institute."

"I think I'm with you," Nate said slowly. "These kids have refused to tell me anything about these robots, but I can make my guesses."

"As could the other generals who were about to arrive at the Combat Force prison. That was another reason for getting them out in a hurry."

"Sir?" I broke in. "What exactly *is* happening? All I know is that we're on a six-day countdown to find the Institute and then rescue my dad from the base. And today is day four."

Cannon glanced at his watch. "A very tight countdown. In a little over 48 hours, the supreme governor and the assembled governors of all the nations of the world will have their annual meeting in New York. It's a simple guess that if the Terratakers are going to try anything, this is the time. Especially if Dr. Jordan believes no one knows he's on Earth and that no one knows about the Institute."

"Impossible to do any damage," Nate scoffed. "You of all people know how tightly secured the meeting will be. Nothing short of the world's best army would be able to get in there."

"Exactly," Cannon returned. "And that's exactly what Jordan has. From what Blaine Steven told us, his army can't be stopped."

The van rounded a corner into a tight canyon.

"Let me correct myself," Cannon added. "Jordan's army can't be stopped without Tyce and Ashley."

"How?" I asked. My knowledge of geography wasn't great, but even I knew that Arizona was a long way from New York.

"I wish I could stop right now and explain it to you," Cannon answered. "But if you look ahead, you'll see our ride." He pointed through the windshield.

We saw a helicopter, painted dull green. Machine guns were mounted on each side.

"I've had the pilot on standby," Cannon said. "Right now every minute counts. You'll learn more when we get to the Institute. I just hope no one tries to shoot us down when we land."

CHAPTER 21

"There?" Cannon shouted a few minutes later.

"There!" Ashley said.

I focused a pair of binoculars where Cannon had pointed. Ahead and below was a box canyon, cut in a perfect square halfway up a mountain. It seemed empty. I truly hoped it was.

I briefly set the binoculars down and glanced around me in the helicopter. Nate squatted on one side, armed with a rocket launcher. Cannon guarded the other side with another rocket launcher. The pilot had his right hand on the trigger mechanisms of the helicopter's machine guns. He was a skinny guy with dark glasses who called himself Grunt. Military people sure liked weird nicknames.

I watched the three of them, tense and ready. If someone attacked as we landed, would we have enough firepower to defend the helicopter?

The helicopter moved in closer, chasing its own shadow across the barren rocks of the desert hills. Slowly it began to take us down into the canyon of the Institute. "Are you sure this is the right place?" Nate asked Ashley.

No one had stepped out of the helicopter yet. We were parked squarely in the middle of the empty canyon. Although the pilot had shut down the helicopter, the roar of the motor echoed in my ears, making the silence around us seem loud.

"I'm sure." Ashley pointed up at the high, narrow mountain peak. "I saw that every day I was allowed out here in the sunshine."

"What," Cannon said to Nate, "you're hoping someone shows up and starts shooting at us?"

"It just doesn't seem right," Nate commented. He had not taken his hands off the rocket launcher. "You'd think if there was something to guard, we wouldn't be able to just walk in like this."

"Fly," Cannon corrected. "It's not like this is easy to get to, even if you know where it is."

Cannon, of course, was right. It had no entrance. This was not a natural canyon but a perfect deep box cut into the rock. Only heavy machinery could have made this. It was too square, the sheer high walls too straight, and the ground too perfectly flat. On the far side, maybe 100 yards from the helicopter, was a large metal door set into the canyon wall.

Nate motioned to the door. "You've been in there, right, Ashley?"

"Every day I was here," she replied. "Inside it's like a maze of rooms. It's where we ate and slept and worked on computer simulations and robot control."

"We've got explosives," Cannon pressed. "We can blow the door apart."

"Then let's do it," Nate said. "We'll leave the kids behind."

I lifted the binoculars again while they began to unload their equipment. I studied the door. There seemed nothing strange about it. Except for the dead lizard on the ground in front of it.

I looked closer, straining my eyes. The lizard seemed to be lying on top of a dead bird. Weird.

I put the binoculars down and said nothing because Nate and Cannon had already begun moving across the open floor of the box canyon. They each carried ready machine guns, with backpacks to carry the explosives.

I peered through the binoculars again.

A tiny mouse scurried up to the dead lizard. Was it going to eat it?

As I watched, the mouse stopped moving. It fell on its side.

Nate's words came back to me. *"You'd think if there was something to guard, we wouldn't be able to just walk in like this."*

"Hey!" I shouted at the two of them. "Hey!" My loud, frantic words bounced off the high rock walls around us.

They stopped.

I waved them back.

"Yes?" Nate asked.

Cannon's eyes didn't settle on me. He was too busy scanning in all directions for danger.

"Remember you thought it was strange that we could just walk in like this?"

Nate nodded.

"Well, what if it *is* guarded? But not by people."

"Trust me," Nate said. "We're keeping our eyes wide open."

"But you haven't been using the binoculars. Try them now. And look at the door from here."

Nate did as I requested. "Dead animals. Place like this, who knows how long they've been there?"

"The mouse just died," I said. "I saw it walk up to the lizard and keel over. I remember reading Earth stories about miners who brought a canary down with them. If it died . . ."

Nate locked eyes with me. "Maybe it was breathing poison gas. Gas leaking out from under the door."

"Exactly," I said. "Who knows what's on the other side of that door?"

"Great," he replied. "So how do we open it without killing ourselves?"

"You don't." I grinned. "Ashley and I do."

CHAPTER 22

"Ready?" Ashley asked.

"Ready," I said.

We sat in the helicopter, each of us plugged in to our bot-packs. Ashley was seat belted in place. Nate had strapped my arms onto my wheelchair. On short notice, it was the best we could do to remain motionless.

One end of the bot-pack was attached to a plug that connected to my spinal nerves. The other end fired X-ray waves to the computer controls on the robot.

The rules of robot control were simple. First, avoid any electrical currents—they could do serious damage to my own brain. Second, disengage instantly at the first warning of any damage to the robot's computer drive. Especially since my brain circuits worked so closely with the computer's circuits.

"Ready for the headset and blindfold," I told Nate.

He placed a soundproof headset on my ears and then a blindfold over my eyes. The fewer distractions to reach my brain in my real body, the better.

It was dark and silent while I waited for a sensation that had become familiar and beautiful to me. The sensation of entering the robot computer.

My wait did not take long. Soon I began to fall off a high, invisible cliff into a deep, invisible hole.

I kept falling and falling and falling. . . .

The morning sun almost blinded me.

It didn't hit my own eyes but one of the four video lenses of the robot parked outside the helicopters.

Beside it was the robot controlled by Ashley. We waved robot arms at each other to confirm we were both in control. Ashley's robot rolled forward.

I followed across the hard-packed sand. For the first time since landing on Earth, I felt like I was in familiar territory. This was no different than traveling across the surface of Mars. To the robot, it didn't feel any different whether the atmosphere around it was oxygen or carbon dioxide.

Or poisonous gas.

Nate had slung a backpack over the right hand of my

robot and given me a quick lesson on how to plant the explosive device.

If I made a mistake and blew it up too early at least it would take off the robot's hand instead of my own.

The door blew perfectly. A green cloud of gas mushroomed outward and dispersed well before reaching the helicopter. We'd been right about a booby trap.

Because Nate and Cannon worried about other traps, they had asked Ashley and me to first explore the inside of the Institute with our robots.

It was dark inside, but that didn't matter. Our robots were equipped with infrared. We didn't need light. And Ashley knew exactly where to go.

We didn't discover any more booby traps.

But we did find light switches.

And 23 kids.

They were in a room just down the hallway.

We halted in shock. Large upright cylinders, made of clear plastic, were almost full of what looked like dark jelly. Wires and tubes ran down from the ceiling into each cylinder.

The 23 kids?

They couldn't talk to us. Couldn't wave at us. Couldn't see us. Or hear us. Each was suspended in one of those cylinders of dark jelly. With only their heads above the jelly and with the tubes and wires running down into their bodies.

Although their eyes were closed, they weren't dead. Only unconscious.

The rest of the Institute was empty. They'd been left behind.

Trapped in life-support systems.

CHAPTER 23

"Put me back!" the first kid pulled from a cylinder shouted. "Put me back!"

Another five minutes had passed since first opening the outer door.

Grunt, our pilot, was still with the helicopter. Nate and Cannon had gone ahead of Ashley and me, once we'd disconnected from our robots, and helped one of the kids out of a cylinder. They'd wrapped him in a blanket.

Ashley had followed me to the room. We had arrived just as the kid woke up and started screaming.

"It's okay," Nate soothed, holding the kid. He was a little bigger than Ashley. His hair was dark and slick where some of that jelly stuff had touched him. "We're friends. We're here to help all of you."

"Put me back!" the kid yelled. His eyes rolled with panic. "If he knows I'm gone, he'll use the death chip! Put me back! Put me back!"

"Son!" Cannon said, leaning over to touch the boy's shoulder. "Son! We can't help you unless you tell us what is happening."

The kid's screams changed to pleading. "Please. Hook me up to my robot. He'll see it isn't responding. He'll think I'm refusing to help. And he'll trigger the death chip."

Ashley stepped forward. "Michael. It's me." She kneeled down beside him and took his hand.

"Ashley, you're back! They said you were dead." Then Michael remembered his panic. "Ashley, tell them to hook me up! You know how we work."

"Michael, we need to know what's happening." Ashley spoke calmly.

"I don't have time to tell you! My robot is down right now. He'll—"

"Dr. Jordan?" Ashley asked.

"Yes! Yes! All of us. He implanted death chips. That's why we do what he tells us. Right now he might be talking to my robot, and if it doesn't respond—" Michael began to sob with fear—"he'll activate the death chip and something in my heart will explode and . . ."

Nate spoke urgently to Ashley. "We really need to know

what's happening here. If he can't tell us, I don't know what to do."

Ashley's eyes narrowed. "Michael, what if I hook up to your robot? Dr. Jordan will have no idea that you and I have switched. These men need to learn everything they can from you."

Michael shivered beneath his blanket. He said nothing for several moments.

Finally he nodded.

"I got to ask you something first," Cannon said. His voice was down to a whisper. "I've looked at all the other kids, and I don't see him. Where's Chad?"

"Chad?" Michael repeated.

"My son," Cannon said. "And someone else. Brian. Both about your age."

"Don't know them," Michael said slowly. I guessed he could tell how worried the general was. "Chad? Brian?"

Cannon bowed his head. "They've got them somewhere else."

Nate put a big hand on the general's shoulder. "Remember, as hostages, they are more valuable alive."

Cannon took a deep breath before lifting his head. "You're right. And here's where we win the first battle in stopping them." He seemed to grow in strength. "Michael, tell us what you can."

"About four days ago," Michael began, "our keepers cleared out of here. Each of us disappeared. Because one by one, they were taking us into this room and hooking us up."

Behind us Ashley was blindfolded and strapped motionless into a chair we'd found. One of the wires from the ceiling was the contact wire to a computer. It had a plug that fit into her spinal plug. The other tubes from the ceiling hung beside her, slowly dripping liquids.

"Hooking you up?" Nate said, as if he were trying to understand the robot-control system.

"All 23 of these kids are controlling robots through virtual reality," I explained. "Robots somewhere away from here."

Michael nodded. "I can't tell you where the robots are, though. I just know that Dr. Jordan is there, supervising us while he waits. But he won't tell us what we're waiting for."

"If the robots aren't here and nearby," Cannon mumbled, more to himself than to Michael, "how can they possibly be controlled?"

"Satellite," I guessed. With my Mars background, I knew a lot about communication technology. "These high mountains are perfect for a transmitter to beam something to a satellite. Signals bouncing at the speed of light from the main computers here could reach anywhere in the world almost instantly."

Cannon's eyes bugged out. "You're telling me these 23 kids are capable of handling their robots anywhere in the world? From this hidden room here?"

"Yes, sir," I said. "I'm afraid that's true."

"It makes sense," Nate commented, stroking his now-stubbled chin. Then he pointed at the other cylinders with motionless kids on life support. "What scares me most is how permanent this looks."

"Permanent?" Cannon asked.

"I'm not a doctor," Nate answered Cannon, "but I do know that when people are in hospitals for long periods, they have to be shifted in their beds at least three times a day. Otherwise they develop horrible bedsores. This jelly stuff . . . it looks like that solves the problem. These kids have been set up in a way that no pressure will be put on their bodies. As long as those tubes supply them with nutrients, they will live in the cylinders indefinitely."

"You can't treat humans like this!" Cannon exploded. "What about sleep?"

"Michael?" Nate asked.

"We all fall asleep at the same time. We all wake up at the same time. And all of us have headaches when we wake. I've talked to some of the other kids—"

"How can you talk to them?" Cannon interrupted. "You're all here, suspended and unconscious on life support."

"Our robots talk to each other," Michael said quietly. "Our bodies might not be moving here, but for 16 hours a day we live through the robot bodies, wherever those bodies are.

Until we fall asleep again. And when we wake up, we see what the robot bodies let us see."

"Must give them some kind of sleeping drug," Nate reasoned. "Drip nutrients through the tubes. And when you want the kids to fall asleep, drip some kind of drug. Measure it right, and they'll wake up eight hours later. If a computer monitors all of this, you don't even need anybody around. Ever."

Cannon made a fist and punched his other palm. "So they've been left here. Like mushrooms. Too afraid to disobey because if they do, Jordan will activate a death chip that kills them in their bodies here."

Michael nodded. "It's worse than that."

"Worse?" Nate asked. "How could this be worse?"

"Here we mostly trained with digging robots. But when they put me in the jelly and I saw through robot eyes on the other side . . ."

"Yes," Cannon said with impatience.

"I was handling a soldier robot. Dr. Jordan is training us on how all of its weapons work. I'm not sure anything can stop these robots."

"Unbelievable," Cannon exclaimed. "These kids are the perfect military weapons. Hidden and untouchable. They control weapons that can be used anywhere in the world. They—"

Ashley suddenly spoke from her chair. "Tyce! Nate! Get me out of this blindfold. I need to talk."

Seconds later, Nate had unstrapped her. She yanked off

her blindfold and blinked a few times. Shaking her hair, she ran her fingers through it.

"Nate," she called frantically, "can you unhook one of the other kids and hook up Tyce? I'm going to need his help. I can't stay here any longer and tell you why. I've got to get back to my robot. Strap me in again."

Without waiting for permission, she pulled her blindfold down again. She slumped back in the chair as she resumed control of her robot.

"Tyce?" Nate asked.

I nodded.

Somewhere in the world was a small army of super-weapon robots. With Dr. Jordan in complete control. I would do everything I could to help Ashley stop him. I wasn't sure how we were going to do it, but I was determined to try. I knew now that Ashley was right. We were the kids' only chance. And now my dad's life hung in the balance too. Even more, what happened in the next 48 hours could change the world—for better or worse.

Five minutes later, I, too, was ready. I was strapped to my wheelchair, blindfolded, and put into a soundproof headset.

I didn't know what was on the other side.

But I was about to find out.

In the darkness and silence, I began to fall . . . fall . . . fall. . . .

JOURNAL
TWO

CHAPTER 1

Smoke bomb!

The only indication of the explosion had been a small crackle and a flash of blinding light. Instead of shock waves of blasting heat, however, dark smoke instantly mushroomed in the warehouse, blocking all light. And sucking out all oxygen.

Like any human, my body and lungs needed oxygen to survive. As the dense, choking smoke filled my vision, I fought panic. If I weren't seeing this through the eyes of a robot, I'd be dead as soon as my lungs ran short of air.

"Targets! Targets! Targets!" a deep voice yelled from somewhere in the smoke. "Kill! Kill! Kill!"

Weird, high-pitched hissing sounds whined past my microphones.

More screaming.

Something—or someone—banged into the hard titanium shell of my robot.

By the clank, I knew I'd been bumped into by another robot. Mine was one of nearly two dozen robots in the room. But that was about all I knew.

I'd connected to this robot body only 30 seconds before. Barely enough time to look around and see the small army of other robots.

Thousands of miles away, the nervous system of my own body was plugged in to a computer that allowed me to control this robot through my own brain waves. I had done that plenty—handled a robot—but not like this before.

Because this robot was different. It rode on wheels, like the one I was used to controlling. But this one was much taller, with four arms. Two arms ended with the normal titanium hands that I'd trained with my entire life. Two others ended in round tubes. I had no idea what to do with those tubes.

The weird hissing sounds continued to buzz overtop in the black confusion of the smoke.

"Ten seconds!" the voice screamed. "Kill! Kill! Kill!"

I made a mental command to switch to infrared vision, something I should have done the instant the smoke mushroomed.

My robot's controls switched away from visual, and the

four video lenses mounted on top of the stem of the robot body blinkered shut.

Temperature sensors gave me instant feedback of my surroundings. What I saw in the shades of blue and orange and red was completely eerie.

The smoke roiled in clouds of cool blue, telling me the bomb had not been a heat detonator nor something intended to explode anything but the smoke. My infrared detected glowing red shapes in the smoke. Human shapes.

"Fifteen seconds! Kill! Kill! Kill!"

Around those red human shapes and me was a frenzy of movement, the faintly red outlines of the titanium shells at room temperature. They scurried back and forth in the smoke. Laser shots zipped from their extended arms, piercing the shading of the smoke.

Laser shots? This was the purpose of the tubes at the end of my extra arms?

I lifted one arm and pointed at the ceiling. I thought out a mental command. *Fire?*

Nothing happened.

I tried another mental command. *Shoot?*

Nothing.

Kill?

It fired. A weird buzzing sound came from my extended arm. My infrared picked up a hot laser that left a tight red glowing circle in the ceiling.

I was shooting!

"Twenty seconds! Kill! Kill! Kill!"

As I began to orient myself and focus better, I saw that the laser beams were going through those human forms, like dozens of blindingly fast arrows zinging through the smoke.

Kill? As in kill people?

Robots spun and circled in all directions. The human shapes ran or crouched or fell. More laser beams. More targets pierced. But where were the screams of dying people?

"Kill! Kill! Kill!"

I scanned with my infrared again. There were only two remaining human figures. One pushed against the far wall, as if it were trying to claw its way out of danger. The other collapsed as I watched.

"Thirty seconds! Kill! Kill! Kill!"

It seemed as if all the robots turned their attention to the red glow of that final human shape against the far wall. Dozens of laser beams zipped toward the upper body, and instantly the shape fell.

"Thirty-three seconds! And stop! Back to visuals."

A giant whoosh began to roar.

I unblinkered my video lenses. I saw fans in the ceiling sucking away the smoke.

As the smoke lifted and the bare walls of the warehouse began to appear beyond the other robots, I looked for all the bodies of the humans who had been shot with laser beams.

Nothing.

Where were the bodies?

I had no time to wonder.

A door opened on the far wall, and a man in a soldier's uniform appeared. "Thirty-three seconds! You are bumbling, pathetic fools!" he shouted through pale, thin lips. He had short blond hair, and his arm and shoulder muscles looked like small, smooth boulders under the tightness of his clothing. His thick neck bulged with veins. "Your opponents were totally blind. And you took over half a minute to kill them."

Kill them? But where were they?

"And you! Number 17!" He strode toward my robot body, pointing a flashlight in his right hand at me. Stopping in front of me, he slapped the flashlight in the open palm of his left hand. "Look above you. Two ceiling holes! Do you think the human soldiers are going to fly to get away?"

I tilted my video lenses up to where he pointed. Little wisps of smoke curled from where I had fired.

"Those were the only two shots you fired." Lifting his cold gray eyes off my robot body, he looked around. "All of you! Each shot you take is monitored by computer. We see exactly what you do."

He directed his next words back to me. "What, you were trying to be merciful? To simulated computer targets?"

I didn't answer. I didn't trust my robot voice to not reveal who I really was—an enemy infiltrator, not the scared kid this man thought he was controlling. I was just glad my actual body was thousands of miles from this terrifying giant.

"When the time comes to kill, you *will* kill! Hear me? Or you will be killed! One flick of a computer switch and your death chip will be activated. Understand?"

He wasn't asking as if he expected an answer. It was a direct command.

"All of you!" he roared to the other robots. "Let Number 17 be an example."

He lifted the flashlight high, like he was going to hit me with it. I almost backed away. Then he lowered it and smiled. "Sweet dreams."

He touched the robot's body stem lightly with the flashlight. That's when I discovered it wasn't a flashlight.

I heard myself scream as an electrical shock ripped through my consciousness.

And I fell into a darkness far blacker than any room filled with smoke.

CHAPTER 2

I woke up seeing the world around me through my own eyes, not the video lenses of a robot. The jolt had disconnected me from the robot body. I now sat in my wheelchair, nowhere near the death-training warehouse or the robot body that had just been delivering information to my brain. The bot-pack was still plugged in to my spine.

What I saw was another windowless room, filled with large, clear cylinders that contained a dark jelly. Two of these 23 cylinders were empty except for the dark jelly. But each of the other cylinders held one kid about my age, with the dark jelly holding them in place. Wires and tubes ran from the ceiling down into the jelly cylinders, connecting to the skulls and arms of each kid. Other tubes removed their body wastes. Only their heads appeared above the jelly. Although their eyes and ears were covered with contoured wax, these kids weren't dead. Only unconscious to the activities around them in this room.

All of them were trapped. Permanently. In 24-hour-a-day life-support systems.

These were the kids running the soldier robots. The kids who had been ordered to kill, kill, kill!

"Stun rod," I said. My words came out as a croak. And my head hurt like it had been sent spinning with a whack from the blunt edge of an ax. I didn't even want to think about how many other times I'd been shocked out of robot contact. Rawling McTigre, my friend on Mars and the director of the Mars Project, had promised that low-level shocks like this wouldn't do any permanent damage.

"Stun rod?" Two anxious faces peered down at me.

"Stun rod." Because I'd been born on Mars and had recently arrived on Earth, I could only guess from memories of all the DVD-gigaroms I'd watched growing up there. "I'm pretty sure that's what happened. He zapped me with a stun rod."

"He? Tyce, who is this 'he' who zapped you?" This question came from the man's face closest to me. It was still out of focus since my head had not stopped its spinning sensation. But I had just traveled with this man for four days. Nate. Nicknamed Wild Man by his platoon buddies in the Combat

Force of the World United Federation. I knew what his face would look like when my vision cleared.

"He. Big he. Mean he. That's all I know about he." I grinned at Nate, even though the extra movement hurt my face. "Am I making sense yet?"

"Why were you zapped? What was happening . . . ?" The other face belonged to General Jeb McNamee. Cannon.

"What was happening on the other side?" I finished for Cannon. One of the top-ranking generals in the Combat Force, he was on this secret mission with us.

Even though the general was up-to-date with all military technology, robot control seemed completely new to him. I think he was still trying to grasp the concept—and its potential. It was almost like he was still in disbelief that my brain waves could be converted into digital signals that bounced off an orbiting satellite into a robot's computer system. I could understand. I'd only found out I had the capability less than a year ago, on Mars.

"Training exercise. At least I think it was. They filled a room with smoke and made all the robots switch to infrared. The targets were . . ." I paused, struggling to make sense of what I'd seen. "The targets must have been simulated by a computer. They were human shaped. With human temperatures. He wanted us to kill them as fast as possible. He was angry it took over 30 seconds."

"What kind of weapons?" Nate demanded.

"How many targets?" Cannon insisted.

I understood their urgency. These were military men. Their job was to stop what was happening on the other side. Only they didn't know exactly where the other side was. Or the real goal of training robot soldiers. Trouble was, neither did I.

"I was in for less than a minute," I reminded them. "And I need to get back or—"

A third voice interrupted me. "—or *I'm* dead."

This voice came from Joey, a kid my age. Wrapped in a blanket, he sat on the floor just beyond Nate and Cannon. Ten minutes earlier, he, too, had been suspended on life support in one of the jelly tubes. We had taken him out of the jelly tube and revived him so I could hook myself up to his robot controls and see what was happening through his robot's eyes.

Joey didn't have to remind me why he'd be dead. Somewhere in his body was the death chip that the giant on the other side had threatened to activate. We didn't know how it worked yet—only that if the kids in the jelly tubes disobeyed their orders, they'd be killed.

"Go back," Joey pleaded. "Please. If Stronsky zapped you, he'll expect you to recover any time now."

Joey pointed at another kid pacing the room at the side of my wheelchair. That was Michael. We had taken him out of a jelly tube too so Ashley could handle his robot. She was now hooked to a bot-pack and sat quietly against the wall, blindfolded so she could totally concentrate on her robot control.

Joey continued. "While you're under, Mike and I will answer as many questions for these guys as possible. But if Stronsky finds out you've replaced me . . ." He lost his voice to his fear.

I understood. If Stronsky—apparently the name of the giant—found out that two of the robots under his control were handled by Ashley and me, he'd activate both Michael's and Joey's death chips. And we would lose any chance of discovering the mission for the robot army. Which meant that those unknown human targets would also die.

"I'm ready to go back," I said. My head still hurt badly, but I had no choice.

"We'll learn what we can here," Cannon said. "You've got to find out what's happening there."

I nodded in return. To prepare for my robot control, I pulled my blindfold down and covered my ears with a soundproof headset.

In total darkness and total silence, I waited for Cannon to reset my bot-pack so I could reconnect with the soldier robot that waited on the other side.

The familiar sensation hit me. As if I were falling off an endless cliff in complete blackness. This was how it always began with robot control. Except this time I had no idea how it would end.

Or if I would make it back.

CHAPTER 3

I emerged out of the darkness to light and sound.

"How was your return to the jelly cylinder, Number 17?" Stronsky growled as the video lenses of my robot opened.

What I saw first were the yellowing teeth of the giant man's wide snarl as he leaned over my robot body. What I heard was the deep rasp of his loud voice.

"Did you like that sensation?" Stronsky shouted. He didn't ask as if he wanted an answer from me. I think he wanted the other robots to hear. They were lined up beside me, so that we formed two rows.

"Did you like finding yourself in jelly up to your neck?" he continued. "Did you like feeling all those tubes in your body? Remember, your body is trapped there. We'll leave it there forever, unless you successfully complete this mission.

Do you want to spend the rest of your life in a jelly cylinder? Do I need to remind you that the system there will support you for 70 years? That's a long time to be stuck staring at a wall."

I knew exactly what he meant. If the life support was automatic—run by a computer—the kids in the jelly tubes would be stuck until they died of old age. And if the computer failed, they would be stuck until they starved to death. Either way, it wasn't good.

"If you don't shape up, you'll get zapped again!" Stronsky yelled at me. He was so worked up that spit flew from his mouth. "Again and again!" He looked up and down the rows of the other robots. "Is that clear to all of you? We have a mission to accomplish, and I want 100 percent effort! You saw what happened to Number 17. I'll do it to any of you at any time. Understand?"

Stronsky's words died to silence in the large, empty warehouse.

Every kid understood. Being trapped for life in a jelly tube was too awful to even think about.

In the quiet, one robot rolled forward, away from the others.

"Who are the targets?" this robot asked. Although the robot speakers somewhat disguised the controller's voice, making it sound tinny and mechanical, I wondered if the speaker was Ashley.

Because Stronsky was directly in front of me, I saw his reaction up close. His eyes widened, his nostrils flared with a quick intake of breath, and then he snorted his anger in shocked disbelief that someone might dare question him.

A moment later the anger faded as pleasure spread across his face. "Number 23," he said softly, "did I hear you right?"

His voice grew louder as he slowly spun in 23's direction. "Did I hear you right? Did I hear you actually ask about our targets? Even after I disciplined Number 8 this morning for asking the same question? How stupid are you?"

It could be no other person than Ashley. She, like me, had not been here earlier to hear the morning's instructions. She, like me, wanted to know the targets so we could get that information back to Nate and Cannon.

"How stupid are you?" he repeated. He slapped his stun gun against his palm as he walked purposefully toward 23. "Stupid enough to wonder what I'm going to do to you now? Let's see if you like a shock as much as 17. Let's see if you like five minutes back in the jelly tube."

Not to Ashley, I thought. *I won't let him.*

I lifted the robot arm and aimed the laser tube at Stronsky. All I wanted to do was hit the stun gun in his hand. With luck, he wouldn't know which robot the shot came from.

All I had to do was think the word *kill* and . . .

I watched closely, waiting for a clear shot.

Here . . . it . . . was . . . and . . . *kill!*

Nothing.

I tried it again. *Kill!* I thought.

Still nothing.

Shoot, I commanded. *Fire. Bang.*

Nothing. Nothing. And nothing.

Another robot arm reached out and yanked my laser tube down.

"Are you crazy?" the robot voice whispered. "You know that the lasers only fire when they've put in their computer code." This was Number 12. All of the robots had bright red numbers on their body stems.

"I've got to stop him," I whispered back.

"And kill all of us? He and Jordan are both wired to our death chip activators. You know the consequences. If their heartbeats stop, so do ours."

"But—"

"What is that noise behind me?" Stronsky roared.

I froze. Number 12 froze.

"That's what I thought," he said, instantly calm again. "No noise. You aren't dumb enough to risk my anger."

This guy was psycho.

Stronsky moved toward 23 again. "Now, my stupid little robot," he said, looking down on the robot that Ashley controlled. Stronsky was a very large man to be able to look down on our robots, which were nearly six feet tall. "It's time you paid the price for your question."

None of the other robots moved. Neither did 23.

"Tempted to try anything to fight back?" Stronsky asked. "After all, you're five times stronger than I am. Your titanium shell is bullet-proof, and I'm only made of muscle and skin. Come on. Try something."

Number 23 rolled forward.

"Death chip," Stronsky said. "Remember? Death chip. Disobey again, and all I have to do is say the word."

If it were Ashley behind Number 23, the death chip would not kill her. No, it would kill the kid she had replaced, a kid who now shivered under a blanket.

Robot 23 stopped.

"That's better," Stronsky said, still slapping his stun gun against his open palm. "Get ready for your medicine."

If she wanted, Ashley could rip him apart. But that would let the people on this end know that she and I had taken over two of their robots. She'd have to let him stun the robot, as if she *were* scared of the death chip.

"Good little robot," Stronsky said. Very slowly he began to lower the stun gun. The look on his face showed he enjoyed the suspense. It showed he enjoyed his sense of control, making the kid controlling the robot wait and wait and wait for the incredible pain of the electric shock.

I wondered if I should step forward and distract Stronsky. Anything to keep him from hurting my friend Ashley.

Stronsky lowered the stun gun, then pulled it back. "Make you flinch?" he taunted 23.

He began to lower it again. Just before I could shout anything, a loud voice reached us from across the warehouse. "No! Enough! I said *train* them, not *damage* them!"

I definitely knew that voice.

I refocused my video lenses on the man stepping out of the doorway. There was no mistaking the round face, round gold-rimmed glasses, and the evil look on his face. It was Dr. Jordan. Who had tried to kill Ashley and me out in space.

He believed we were dead.

I was afraid to think what might happen once Dr. Jordan found out we were still alive.

And now among his robot soldiers.

CHAPTER 4

"What seems to be the difficulty here?" Dr. Jordan asked in an intimidating tone. He walked quickly across the warehouse floor and was soon eye to eye with Stronsky. "Let me repeat," Dr. Jordan said fiercely. "What seems to be the difficulty here?"

Despite his gigantic size, Stronsky looked terrified.

I understood. I'd faced Dr. Jordan's wrath before.

"I am applying discipline techniques," Stronsky said, his voice shaking. "You weren't here, and I know how important it is that all of these robots learn to obey instantly."

"Well, I'm here now," Dr. Jordan snapped. "So tell me who needed discipline and why."

"Number 17 decided to show mercy to his targets during a computer simulation of tomorrow's attack. He shot the ceiling instead of our heat figures."

Dr. Jordan turned his eyes on me. It felt like he was looking right through the robot body and seeing me controlling it in my wheelchair. "I see," he said. "And Number 23?"

"Perhaps the opposite problem," Stronsky said. "Number 23 was eager to find out who tomorrow's targets were."

"Perhaps we can forgive Number 23," Jordan said with a sinister smile. "I like a bloodthirsty robot. But I am troubled by Number 17. You applied shock treatment?"

"Yes," Stronsky answered.

Dr. Jordan strode toward me. He tapped his chin as he stared at me thoughtfully. "Did you learn your lesson, Number 17?"

Even though I knew the robot's speakers would alter my real voice, I was afraid to speak.

"Answer me!"

"I learned my lesson," I said.

Dr. Jordan let out a loud sigh. "Perhaps now is the time to let you know something." He stepped backward so he could survey all the robot soldiers. "I know all of you have believed since childhood that you are orphans."

All of us except for me. Because I'd been born on Mars, I was the only one among the kids who controlled these robots not to have been raised in the Institute—back where they were now held prisoners in jelly tubes. But because of my friendship with Ashley—who had been raised with the others before she was brought to Mars for the Hammerhead mission

—I knew what Dr. Jordan said was true. Ashley had told me that both of her parents had died in a car crash. The only things she had left from them were two silver cross earrings. She'd given one of them to me as a symbol of our friendship.

"In one way, it does make sense that we would use orphans for these robot experiments," Dr. Jordan continued. "Who cares about you? Who would come looking for you? The secret military arm responsible for the operations that gave you robot control would naturally pick experimental test subjects who have no family ties."

He paused for dramatic effect. "So let me give you some good news. We have lied to you from the beginning. Your parents are not dead."

A low, excited buzzing filled the warehouse. It took me a moment to realize it was the voices of the robots. With the exception of Ashley and me, the kids who controlled them were each stuck in their jelly tubes back at the Institute. There, even though they were inches apart, they were on life support and could not communicate by the use of their human voices and human ears. The only life they now led was through the robot bodies, and they could only talk among themselves here on this side. Now they were acting no differently than if they had gathered in a schoolyard.

"Silence!" Dr. Jordan roared. "Silence!"

The buzzing and talking instantly stopped.

"Let me now give you the bad news," he said softly. His

voice carried clearly. All the others, I guess, were as afraid of him as I was. "Yes, your parents are alive. For now."

The silence seemed to become even more silent—if that were possible—as the kids controlling the robots listened intently through the robot audio controls.

"Yes, we can kill you through the death chip. All of you knew that going into this little military exercise. But now you need to know something more. We can—and will—also kill your parents if you disobey. And your brothers and sisters. Wherever they are in the world."

Dr. Jordan rubbed his goatee as he stared at the robots gathered in front of him. "Think of yourselves as valuable hostages. Your parents are in positions of power, and they are held helpless because they are afraid of us hurting you. But now you must think of your parents as hostages and fear us hurting them. Wonderful, is it not, how we get so much use out of you?"

The silence remained.

"Good," he said. "Very good that all of you are wise enough not to comment. I expect then that my commands will be obeyed instantly and without question." He pointed to the open door at the far end of the warehouse. "Follow me. The first one to make any noise will be immediately punished by Stronsky."

Without looking to see if he was being followed, Dr. Jordan spun on his heels and walked toward the door. Stronsky stepped in behind him.

I rolled into line behind the other robots.

Like the perfect army, we followed.

And that was what was most terrifying of all. For the first time in the history of mankind, we *were* the perfect army.

Undefeatable.

CHAPTER 5

I have never seen a real praying mantis—only a picture of one on the DVD-gigaroms that showed me everything I knew about Earth before I actually got here. In a way, I think our army of robots must have looked like a line of those stick insects. Except, of course, for the lower half, which had an axle that connected two wheels. Turning the robot was simple. If one wheel moved forward while the other moved backward, it could spin instantly.

The robot's upper body, however, did look like a praying mantis. It was sticklike, with a short, thick, hollow pole that stuck upward from the axle. A heavy weight counterbalanced the arms and head. Within this weight was the battery that powered the robot, with wires running up inside the hollow pole to the head parts.

I was familiar with my own robot, the one I had trained with on Mars. I assumed these were based on a nearly identical design, except for the extra two arms that fired the lasers.

I knew that robots were perfect for exploring Mars. But it wasn't until now that I realized robots also made perfect soldiers.

They were strong—their titanium hands could grip a steel bar and bend it.

They were fast—their wheels moved three times faster than any human could sprint.

Bullets wouldn't stop them. Smoke or poison gas wouldn't stop them. Bombs wouldn't kill them. Not with the kids controlling them hundreds or thousands of miles away.

The big question was very simple. What did Dr. Jordan intend to do with this perfect army?

"Into the truck," Dr. Jordan commanded.

For five minutes we as robots had followed him and Stronsky down a brightly lit corridor. The only noise had been the sound of our wheels squeaking against the floor.

At the end of the corridor Dr. Jordan had pushed a button and a large door had slid open.

It was dark beyond, but after my vision adjusted, I realized it was the inside of a truck trailer, backed up to the warehouse.

"No talking," he said as we filed past him. "None. Not even a whisper."

It was an unnecessary warning. I would have guessed that all the kids were thinking about what they had just learned. Their parents were still alive.

Ashley hadn't talked about it much, but it was easy to imagine how often she would have wondered what it might be like to grow up with a real family. I wondered what she was thinking now, knowing her parents were alive. Knowing Ashley and how responsible she felt for this mission, I figured she'd shove that news to the back of her mind until we'd rescued the other kids and stopped Dr. Jordan.

Their parents are still alive. If these kids did something wrong with their robots, though, their parents might die.

I understood that too. Although my mother was still under the dome on Mars, my father was here on Earth. In a Combat Force prison. Waiting for Ashley and me to rescue him.

I couldn't make mistakes either, or I would lose him, just as surely as if Dr. Jordan had him killed.

I rolled onto the truck with the other robot soldiers.

"Face me," Dr. Jordan ordered from the inside of the warehouse.

Each of us spun our robot bodies quickly.

"Good, good," he said. "See what a little incentive will do for you?"

No one answered.

"We're going to shut the trailer door now. Don't worry about getting bored during your trip." Dr. Jordan took a small remote control out of his pocket. He pressed a button on it and cocked his head as he listened for a beep that told him the signal had been sent successfully.

I wondered where. But when I heard his next words, I understood. It controlled the computers back at the Institute.

"Sleep time, boys and girls," Dr. Jordan said, "A long sleep. Until the day after tomorrow, which is going to be a big day."

Sleep time. We knew from Michael and Joey that the computer controlling the life-support system sent sleeping drugs into the kids' bodies through the nutrient tubes hooked up to them. The kids fell asleep instantly in their jelly tubes when the drugs hit. It was like shutting them off. In the morning, different drugs would be pumped in to wake them up. It was sad. The kids controlled machines, and yet their bodies had been turned into machines. Dr. Jordan could make them sleep as long as he wanted, then wake them up at his convenience.

It really made me angry that the kids were so helpless. After all, Dr. Jordan was manipulating them, controlling everything about their lives. Making them prisoners in these jelly tubes. And he was doing it through fear. It wasn't right.

It helped that Ashley and I had at least one secret weapon against Dr. Jordan. Because Ashley and I weren't hooked up to the nutrient tubes, we wouldn't be sleeping.

As the door to the truck trailer began to slide down, Dr. Jordan turned to say something to Stronsky.

I amplified the hearing controls of the robot's audio. Above the suddenly loud squeaking of the closing door, I clearly heard their conversation.

"Numbers 17 and 23 were our best students," Dr. Jordan said. "I'm very puzzled that you had problems with them."

"They won't make trouble anymore," Stronsky said. "Nothing like a good shock to—"

"Go easy on the shock treatment," Dr. Jordan interrupted sharply. "These kids are worth billions each. They are irreplaceable as military weapons. We must do nothing to endanger their lives. I want you to check them out immediately."

"Check them out? They're in the trailer with—"

"Not the robots, idiot. The kids themselves. Run a satellite check and monitor their bodies. I want to make sure all of their body functions are fine."

If a robot body had blood, mine would have frozen.

I knew what Dr. Jordan didn't. Back on the other side, two of the kids were not on life support anymore. The computer monitor would pick up no vital signs from either of them. Once Dr. Jordan discovered this, he'd have some serious questions about exactly who was controlling the robot bodies of 17 and 23.

"Ashley!" I hissed into the darkness. Her robot was

somewhere among the others packed into the back of this truck. "Ashley!"

"Tyce?"

"We have to go back," I said. "Now!"

CHAPTER 6

Ashley beat me back. More accurately, she was quicker than I was in removing her blindfold and headset. For each of us, all it took to leave robot control was a quick mental shout of the word *Stop!*

So, as I lifted my blindfold, she was already standing in front of me, hands poised on her hips in typical Ashley fashion.

She flashed me the grin that always made me feel warm. When she tucked a lock of straight black hair behind her right ear, I saw the flash of her silver cross earring.

Nate and Cannon stood behind her.

"What's happening?" Cannon asked.

"Plenty." I repeated what I'd heard. "You know they're using a computer to automatically handle the jelly tubes. Stronsky is about to monitor it remotely any minute now."

"Explain . . ." Cannon's forehead crinkled with concern. "With everything I've been learning today, I think I can guess. But I learned a long time ago not to make assumptions."

I could see the spark in Ashley's almond-shaped eyes as she explained for Cannon's benefit. "If signals are being sent from us here off a satellite to the robots, it wouldn't be hard for them to use the same satellite to get information on their end from a computer here."

She was right. Not too far away, back on the helicopter that had taken us here, was my comp-board. It would be no problem for Dr. Jordan and Stronsky to use one like it to check the computer that ran the life support.

"What's to monitor?" Cannon asked. "I mean, how could they know if any of the kids are disconnected from the jelly cylinders?"

"Brain-wave activity?" I asked.

Michael spoke up. "Through our spinal plugs. We're able to send our brain waves out to control the robots, so I'm sure they'd be able to do it in reverse. If the spinal plug is in place, they might be able to read our brain-wave activity through it."

All of us glanced at the two empty jelly cylinders and then the others, each filled with a kid on life support. Michael had been in one. Joey, who now watched us carefully, had been in the other.

"Don't put me back in," Michael begged. "It's horrible. The only thing you can move is your eyeballs."

"There's only a couple of seconds each day when we reconnect from sleep on this end to the robot on the other," Joey said, sounding panicked. "Those two seconds . . . it feels like I'm trapped forever. How can you ask us to go back in and just wait until all of this is over?" He began to cry.

I didn't know what to say. If Dr. Jordan found out what was happening here, we wouldn't have a chance of stopping him. But how could we force these kids back into the jelly cylinders after all they'd been through?

"There's something you should know," Ashley said to Joey and Michael. "Dr. Jordan told us our parents are alive." Her voice stopped there, as if she were choking back a sob.

"What!" Joey stopped crying.

Michael's jaw dropped. "Alive?"

"He's using that against us as a threat," Ashley said. "But once we find a way to stop him, we can look for our parents. Right?"

"He's planted death chips in all of us," Joey said. "If we don't listen to him, he kills us. And if he dies, the chips are activated automatically. How could we ever stop him?"

"I don't know," Ashley said. "At least not yet. But I do know the only chance we have is to fool him into thinking you're both still hooked up. Then Tyce and I can go back and do our best."

Silence.

"Here's something," I said quietly. "We won't have to put you back in the jelly cylinders. Just get you hooked up again."

"I'll do it," Michael said firmly. "Plug me back in."

"Me too," Joey said, although he had to take a gulp of air. "For as long as it takes."

"It shouldn't be long," I said. I knew the kids were making a big sacrifice, going back to their worst nightmare. "We'll give Stronsky a half hour to run his check on you. But we've got to move fast."

Cannon and Nate rushed to reconnect both kids.

Ashley stared at the other rows of jelly cylinders. "Tyce," she said softly, "follow me."

I rolled my wheelchair forward.

Slowly we passed cylinder after cylinder. Each cylinder showed the darker outline of a kid's body stuck in the dark, thick jelly, with the liquid pushing against the thin clothing they wore. Clear liquids slowly dripped through the clear plastic tubing that had been placed in their veins. I'd once thought Mars food was tasteless. Now I wondered what I'd ever complained about. These kids didn't get to eat a single meal. All the vitamins and nutrients they needed to live long, healthy lives reached their blood directly through the veins in their arms.

Most frightening of all, however, were the faces that we passed. Each kid's eyes were closed, and the wax plugs quivered as their eyeballs moved slightly, as if they were dreaming. Or fighting nightmares.

I heard a slight noise. It took me a couple of seconds to realize Ashley was crying.

"I *hate* this," she said. "When we were growing up here in the Institute, none of us knew they had *this* in mind for us. They were getting us ready, like cows for slaughter. Except this is worse than death. They can only live through their robots."

I touched Ashley's hand and gripped it. I hadn't grown up in the Institute, so I couldn't fully feel her pain. But I shared her anger and confusion. How could I help her through what I couldn't understand myself?

Ashley continued to cry quietly. "It seems forever since I left here. It wasn't bad, you know. We thought we were orphans. We were learning to run robots. And none of us knew why. But while I was gone, they put everyone into these cylinders. . . ." She turned away and swiped at her cheek. "I feel so guilty. If I hadn't been sent to Mars, I'd be in one too."

It was true. Ashley *had* escaped this fate because she'd been sent to run some secret experiments on the Hammerhead torpedo. One that would have been controlled like any other robot. One that would have given Dr. Jordan and his Terrataker rebels the capability to kill millions. Only Ashley's bravery had stopped him.

"Someone else might not have survived," I told her. "You did. And returned. It's the only chance the kids have. So if you hadn't been sent to Mars . . . if you hadn't crashed the

Hammerhead . . . if you hadn't helped us figure out what was happening to the *Moon Racer* . . . It's almost like God planned for you to be here."

Ashley placed a hand on my shoulder. "Thanks."

Suddenly she tightened her grip. "Tyce, I don't believe what I see."

CHAPTER 7

Ashley stared hard into a cylinder.

"I don't believe this." She moved down the row and stared into another cylinder. Then another. "I really don't believe this."

Before I could roll forward in my wheelchair and catch up with her, she returned. "I know all the kids I grew up with. We all learned robot controls here, hidden away from the world. Most of us arrived when we were five or six years old. Old enough to remember our parents."

Ashley drew a deep breath, like she was trying to keep herself from crying again. Then she let the breath out. I could tell she didn't want to talk any more about her parents.

"See, Tyce," she said, "I think they needed to take us when we were that young. The spinal-plug operations probably won't work on older kids who have already done a lot of their growing."

That made sense. I knew my own operation had happened before I could remember.

"And if that is true," Ashley continued, "it makes sense that the younger the kid is, the easier the spinal nerves can grow into the virtual-reality control system."

"Sounds right."

"I'm wondering," she said, "if it's also easier to train kids the younger they are. I was 10 by the time my spinal plug had grown into my nervous system. And after that, it took me a couple of years to learn the robot controls because I kept mixing them up with my own muscle movements."

"That makes sense too," I replied. On Mars, I'd spent years and years in virtual-reality training sessions before anyone even told me I was capable of robot control.

"I was afraid of that." Ashley walked forward a few more paces. I followed.

She pointed at the last few jelly cylinders, the ones she had stared into.

At first, I didn't understand. The jelly was so thick that it hardly let any light into the center, where the kids were suspended.

Then, with horror, I realized what she meant. And what she couldn't believe.

Behind us, all of the kids had been close to her age. Not these kids at the end.

"Ashley," I said slowly, "these kids here are—"

"I know everyone in all the other cylinders," she said. "I know their faces as if we were brothers and sisters. I've never seen these kids before. And they can't be more than eight years old!"

A shiver ran down my spine. She was right. They did look like eight-year-olds. With faces much younger than the kids in the other jelly cylinders. Tiny, innocent faces with eyes closed.

It made me sick. My anger grew until I thought it would burst. Dr. Jordan was treating these kids as if they weren't even human. Like they were cows or monkeys in a test lab. Using them as slaves to do his bidding. Not giving them even the chance to experience life outside a jelly tube. In the early 21st century, all such experiments, even with animals, had been banned. And yet they'd still been going on—with humans this time—right under the World United Federation's nose. Worse, the experiment was being run by one of their own top Combat Force people.

I voiced out loud the thought I didn't want to say. "Are you telling me that half the kids you grew up with aren't here? And that they've been replaced by these younger kids you don't know?"

"Yes," Ashley stated flatly. In the light her face looked a little green.

When we had first arrived in this room, General Cannon had frantically searched all the cylinders, looking for his own son who had supposedly been kidnapped and taken to the Institute. I now understood why he hadn't found him.

"That can mean only one thing," I said, pointing at the rows of jelly cylinders. "This isn't Dr. Jordan's only army."

CHAPTER 8

"I think we wait one hour," Cannon said wearily to Ashley
and me. "By then, Jordan and Stronsky should have finished
their monitoring. Then it will be safe to unhook those two
boys and let you replace them again. We desperately need you
controlling robots on the other side. Otherwise we're totally
blind to Jordan's operation."

Cannon's face looked older than it had earlier that morning—before we'd found our way into this place in the Arizona
desert mountains. As if defeat had taken away his strength.
I thought of the younger kids Ashley and I had just left behind
us to return to the general. And I thought I understood why he
looked so defeated. Another kid. His son, Chad. It must be ter-
rible to think about him trapped in a jelly tube—somewhere.
And not to be able to find him or get to him.

"General?" I said. "I remember the first thing you did when we got here. You looked for your son. You asked Michael and Joey about him."

Cannon nodded. "I was hoping so much I'd find him here. . . ."

Some things were slowly beginning to make sense. Dr. Jordan had said all the parents of these kids were in positions of power, so that the kids could be used as hostages. Cannon was in a high position in the Combat Force. And besides the president of the World United Federation, no one in government held a higher position than the supreme governor, who had sent Cannon to help Ashley and me. And he was missing his grandson, Brian.

"I'm not sure if this is good news or bad news," I said. "But your son may be in another group."

"Like this?" Cannon's eyes widened.

"I don't know if that group is in jelly cylinders like this one," I replied, "but it's beginning to look like these aren't the only kids with robot control."

Once, not very long ago, I'd thought I was the only kid in the solar system wired to handle a robot. Later I'd thought Ashley was the only other kid. Then I'd learned about an entire Institute of kids like us on Earth. So now it didn't seem so impossible that there could be more than one group.

When I paused, Ashley quickly explained that half the kids in these jelly cylinders were strangers to her.

"You're saying that part of this group has been sent away, with replacements added?" the general's voice boomed. "That there are more than 24 kids with robot control?"

Ashley nodded. "So maybe Chad is among them."

"But how many groups can there be?" Nate said. He had been pacing in small circles around us, listening intently. "Each one of them might be equipped as an army, just like this one."

"I'm afraid Jordan had access to substantial amounts of funding," Cannon said, shaking his head. "He was one of the top robot scientists in the Combat Force. We all thought . . ." He put his face in his hands, then sighed as he rubbed his hands back and forth. "It's no coincidence that I'm here. Since we've got to wait anyway, we've got time for me to explain Earth politics."

We listened. Some of it I knew. Some of it was new to me.

Twenty years earlier, the mushrooming population of Earth had made it obvious that horrible things were ahead for mankind. Countries were on the verge of war in their desperate search for enough water and energy. All the statistics and research showed that a threshold of efficiency had been reached. Within a century all the available resources would not be enough to support the projected population, let alone continued growth. A third world war was inevitable. With nuclear weapons available to most countries, it would be a war that might cause human extinction.

While many solutions were proposed, only two became popular. And these two caused a growing political divide.

One side called for expansion beyond Earth. Instead of limiting population, they said we should find new places for humans. Like the Moon, where a small colony had already been established under domes. And on Mars, where the dream was to make an entire new planet available for people to live outside of domes.

The other side called for drastic reduction of growth. Instead of spending valuable resources to find room for more people, they said we should limit the population and raise the quality of life.

The most difficult issue was a simple phrase: *drastic reduction of growth*. Which meant proposed solutions like a lottery for licenses that would allow parents to have children. And putting to death "undesirable" people who were disabled, terminally ill, or simply too old. In a Terrataker world, someone like me might simply be eliminated.

As the issue was debated and voted upon, country after country rejected mandatory population control, because that meant allowing government decision makers to play God with people's lives. The choice was made to find new places for people to live, which would only be possible if all the countries in the world joined in this common goal.

This began the next major political debate. World leaders sought a way to make a common political goal possible, without any country losing independence. In the end, the former United Nations became the World United Federation. A 100-year treaty was enacted among all the countries of the world, with a common pledge of resources and technology to the goal of space expansion.

This was not a one-world government, however, with a common currency and one leader. No, the political structures within each country remained unchanged. Each country elected and sent one governor to the World United Federation Summit, which met twice yearly to promote continued peace and the urgent long-term goal of the treaty.

This established the commitment of the world to the Mars Dome.

Yet the highly passionate debate over expansion versus population control left a ticking time bomb within this new world political structure. It was costing billions to support the Mars Dome, and many were angry about the higher taxes needed for this. Within each country, some of the fiercest opponents of space expansion banded together. They called themselves Terratakers, for all they wanted was the Earth alone. And the right to choose who should live and die. As a political group, they made trouble often. But when it became apparent that they could not change the resolve of the majority by democratic means, they turned to terrorism.

CHAPTER 9

"Terrorism," I said, echoing Cannon's last word. I'd nearly died in space because of that terrorism. And before that, I had seen the results on Mars.

"Terrorism," General Cannon repeated solemnly. "And among that, kidnapping." His voice dropped. "But not highly public kidnappings for ransom. Secret kidnappings. Over a period of years, they took children of men and women who had influence in the government and military. Even those parents didn't realize the kidnappings had taken place."

"I don't understand," I said. "How—?"

"I thought Chad had drowned in a boating accident," the general said. "The river was searched for days, and the experts said we shouldn't expect to find his body. We had a funeral for him. It was one of the most difficult days of my life. And then . . ."

Cannon's voice broke. "I'll never forget the man's face that day in D.C. So ordinary, like any other person stopping me on the street to ask for directions. But there was something horrible in his eyes that chilled me. He asked if I'd ever like to see my son again. Before I could even begin to show my anger at his disrespect for our family's grief, he held up a photo, with my son holding that day's newspaper. Then he told me the rest."

He drew a breath. "I imagine it's what the other parents were told. If I let anyone else know Chad was alive, even my wife, they would kill him. Same thing if I let anyone know he was being held hostage. Or if I searched for him. He told me my son was safe and growing up well protected, and that it would stay that way. He promised I would see him in a couple years, and in the meantime, someone might occasionally ask me for a favor. He said if I wanted Chad to live, I'd be wise to give that favor. Then the man walked away and disappeared in the crowd on the street. That was it."

Cannon lifted his hands with a helpless shrug. "What could I do? Too little. I'm one of the highest-ranking Combat Force generals, and I was as powerless as a baby to help my little boy. Then I heard about a senator on the other side of the country whose daughter wandered away in the woods during a picnic and was never found. And about a governor of a country in Africa who had a son taken by a lion, but the body was never found. And someone from Russia who had a son and daughter die in a fire, but the police were unable to identify any remains. Each of them had been extremely pro-Mars, and suddenly each, in their own political systems, began voting against money for the dome. That told me a lot. Even then, with my suspicions, I didn't dare ask questions or begin to look for Chad in any way. I couldn't even tell my wife our son was alive, even though she was sick with grief."

Cannon stopped for a long time, staring at the far wall.

"The favor . . . ," Nate said.

"Favor?"

"Did anyone ever come to you?"

"Yes," Cannon said dully. "TFT. Tactical Future Technology. A top secret research program. I report directly to the president of the United States. Two years ago, when it looked like funding was going to run dry for TFT, I received a note that told me to make sure the money continued to flow for it and to petition the president for it. And I'm talking billions of dollars unknown to the public. I guess they knew I was upset at how some things had gone wrong since I first helped begin that same program."

He snorted bitterly. "After all, when a little-known scientist had approached me with the idea, I'd been one of the first to see the potential of this new technology. And the first to convince our country's president he should go to the Federation's supreme governor to create the secret TFT program. You see, after the prolonged political battles with the Terratakers about mandatory population control, it was obvious the public would be against trying experiments on humans that had only worked on monkeys. But I thought this robot technology would be used for space exploration."

"General?" Nate prompted when Cannon lapsed into silence again.

Cannon's lips were tight with anger as he spoke. "That was 14 years ago. Because of my military ranking, the president listened to me. The dome had been established on Mars, and the second spaceship was about to leave Earth. Because of me, the president and the supreme governor arranged for a neural specialist to be on that ship. His assignment was to perform an operation on someone on Mars. An operation that had never been performed on any human. Mars was perfect. We could control the information that reached Earth. And . . ."

In a flash, I knew what he was going to say. So I finished it for him. "It just so happened that there was one person on Mars young enough that the bioplastic fibers implanted into his spinal column would have a chance to fuse as he grew."

"I had the best intentions, Tyce," Cannon said to me with great sadness. "They told me the operation would not fail. That they had performed it on hundreds of monkeys. But they didn't tell me that all those operations had taken place in a controlled environment, with teams of doctors surrounded by millions of dollars of technology. On Mars, when something went wrong . . ."

Again, Cannon couldn't finish his sentence. I was in my wheelchair, directly in front of him. That said enough about what had happened during the operation.

I felt my anger growing. This was the man who had made an order that changed my life forever. Who had given him that right?

Cannon found the strength to mock himself with a smile. "In a real way, I've already been punished. Because that little-known scientist who approached me put the secret TFT money into research no one in the highest level of government ever expected." He lifted his arms, taking in the jelly tubes that surrounded us. "Like this."

One last sigh from the general. "In a way, I got the punishment I deserved. My son was taken from me by people paid with money that I had convinced our president to approve on the TFT. Because that little-known scientist was Dr. Jordan. We sent him to Mars, posing as an artificial-intelligence expert. But he was the founder of robot control technology. And I discovered far, far too late that he was one of the Terratakers."

CHAPTER 10

With Cannon beside me, I wheeled into the cool air of an
evening in the desert mountains. The helicopter that had
brought us here was parked ahead on flat, packed ground.
Behind us in the sheer rock face of this hidden Arizona valley was the doorway that led to the rooms of the Institute.
And above, the stars pierced the growing darkness of the sky,
filling me with a longing for Mars, unreachable all those millions and millions of miles away.

I thought of Mom and the experiments she was doing to
find a way to grow plants that could live on Mars. I wondered
how she'd react when she found out it was this man who had
pushed the funding that put me in a wheelchair. I knew she
would tell me to soften my anger at him, something I didn't
want to do. I wanted to tell her all the other things that had

happened to me on Earth. How beautiful it was. How scared I was with Dad in prison, waiting for Ashley and me to return.

I realized I was homesick. For Mars and for my memories of growing up under the dome. I would only get there again with my dad if Ashley and I somehow found a way to stop Dr. Jordan.

Cannon said nothing as we crossed the short distance to the helicopter. Maybe he was wondering, too, how we might stop Dr. Jordan. More likely, Cannon was angry that we were headed back to the helicopter.

"I don't like this," he said, breaking his silence as we neared the helicopter. "I don't like that you won't tell me why you want to do this. I don't like the way you've given me no choice."

Part of it was because of my anger. I was taking silent satisfaction in pushing him around. But I had another reason for forcing him to listen to me.

A few minutes ago—right after he'd told us about his involvement with Dr. Jordan—I had asked for the general's password to his e-mail account and access to the Internet through the helicopter's computer system. When I refused to tell him why, Cannon had said no. So I had informed him that, unless he allowed it, I would not handle the robot on the other side for him. I had been bluffing, of course. Along with everything else, my dad's life depended on Ashley's and my success.

"Last chance," Cannon barked as we stopped at the helicopter. "Why are you doing this? Do you have any idea what you are asking to be able to access my e-mail account?"

"Sir," I said, stone-faced, "I've already explained. I'll be able to tell you later."

He stared at me and must have seen that I wouldn't change my mind.

"Grunt," Cannon shouted to the helicopter pilot, "help us on board." Then he turned to me and spoke softly, "Don't forget that I've already explained something to you too. One simple fact. We don't have much time."

I didn't need the reminder.

From: "General Jeb McNamee"
<mcnameej@combatforce.gov>
To: "Rawling McTigre" <mctigrer@marsdome.ss>
Sent: 03.30.2040, 10:31 p.m.
Subject: Please read this right away!

Rawling,

Even though this e-mail is coming from General McNamee, it's me. Tyce. Here's how you can know: On the trip you and I and Dad made from the dome to search for the evidence of an alien civilization, I bumped the robot's head underneath the platform buggy as I was trying to fix the flat tire. Remember? And I asked you what kind of pill to take for a robot headache. It was a dumb remark, but Dad was outside in his space suit, so only you and I would know about it.

You're probably wondering why I need to prove it's me. And how and why I've logged on to the e-mail account of a general in the Combat Force of the World United Federation.

Here's the "why" first. It's because I'm not sure you've received any of my e-mails since I left Mars. I'm also not sure if any of the e-mails you sent me actually came from you.

I can't give you all the details now, but you know that I always keep a journal of things that happen to me. With this e-mail, I'll be attaching my journal of the entire trip from Mars to Earth in the Moon Racer and you'll learn about the last person you would have ever suspected to be helping the Terratakers.

The short story is that he was able to secretly access the mainframe computer under the dome. From the time the dome was established! That meant he was able to monitor and change all incoming and outgoing reports and e-mails from Mars to Earth and from Earth to Mars. Most of what you reported about the genetic experimentation, alien civilization, and the Hammerhead *space torpedo didn't even reach Earth. We only thought it did, because of the fake e-mails sent back to the dome.*

I stopped and thought of Rawling reading this in his office. He'd probably be sitting forward, leaning toward the computer screen in shock, instead of his usual feet-propped-up-on-the-desk habit. I could just see him—his short, dark hair streaked with gray, his wide shoulders that showed he used to be a quarterback on Earth. Although he was in his mid-forties, he was one of my best friends and one of two medical doctors under the dome.

I could just see his office too. I smiled. It was the only one under the dome that had framed paintings of Earth scenes, like sunsets and mountains, on the walls. Rawling hated them, because of what they represented. Blaine Steven, the previous director, had spent a lot of the government's money to get those luxuries included in the expensive cargo shipped to Mars. I bet Rawling still hadn't gotten around to taking them down yet. He always had more pressing matters, like all the life-and-death crises we'd been faced with on Mars recently.

What Rawling might not know yet was that the communications had been controlled from Mars since the beginning. So we on Mars would only get the information that Dr. Jordan and the other Terrataker rebels wanted us to have. And so even the highest-level World United Federation leaders on Earth would only have select information about Mars.

It was incredibly simple and incredibly smart to control all the outgoing and incoming messages and reports on the dome. After all, with Mars 50 million miles from Earth, those communications were the only way to stay in touch. We had no way of knowing that any reports reaching us were lies. And vice versa, with the stuff being sent back to Earth. Who knew how much damage the Terratakers had done this way?

I thought about it and began to type again.

In other words, you may have sent me dozens of e-mails, and I wouldn't know it if someone intercepted them and wrote back as if he were me. Same with the messages I sent you.

I know that to be true because in one of my e-mails I tested you by making a mistake on purpose, and it wasn't corrected. Since then, Dad and I and Ashley almost got fried by getting sucked into the sun, got arrested on Earth after we managed to rescue ourselves, and then Ashley and I were forced to leave Dad behind in a Combat Force prison as we went searching for the other Institute kids. This has been my first chance to send you an e-mail.

I'm doing it from what I think is the safest channel for three reasons. First, to let you know we've made it safely so far. Dr. Jordan found a way to escape, and it will take a complete journal to tell you what's been happening, and I don't have the time. If I get back to you tomorrow, you'll know we stopped him. If not . . .

I lifted my fingers from the keyboard again. We had to stop Dr. Jordan. But there was a big difference between knowing what we had to do and figuring out a way to do it. To me, Dr. Jordan and the army of robot soldiers seemed unbeatable. Especially since he had the power of the death chip to control the kids in the jelly tubes.

Thinking about it, I wanted to give up. But if I had learned anything from Rawling, my mom, and my dad, it was that giving up was never an option.

. . . if not, I don't know when I'll get a chance to send you another e-mail. And that's my second reason for sending this. To let you know that the mainframe computer has been tampered with and that you need to make sure all the communications with Earth haven't been tampered with. (If you don't get this, of course, that means someone else is still intercepting communications, and you'll never know anyhow, but this was the best I could do.)

Third reason? I just want to know that you and Mom are doing fine. I miss you both. A lot. And I pray for you

every day. Please send an e-mail back to the general's
account, not mine. And please do it right away, because I'll
check for mail in a couple of hours. I'll know it's you when
you tell me what dumb joke you made in return that day
when I made my dumb joke about the robot's headache.

Really hoping to hear from you.
Your friend,
Tyce

I saved the e-mail. Then I made a quick copy of my *Moon Racer* journal and attached it to the e-mail before I hit the send button. Although electronic transmissions traveled at the speed of light, it would take a while for the e-mail to travel those 50 million miles and reach the dome's mainframe on Mars.

I wished I could have told Rawling the fourth and most important reason I had sent him that message. But I didn't want to risk revealing it in case someone was monitoring the e-mails.

Right now my life, my dad's life, Ashley's life, and the lives of all the Institute kids depended on Cannon. Yet he was the same guy who had long ago ordered the operation that put me in a wheelchair. The same guy who had been working with Dr. Jordan for years.

Now I wasn't sure if I could trust Cannon. Maybe he had lied about having a son taken hostage. Maybe he was just stringing Ashley and me along.

It would make me feel a lot better if this e-mail went through. If people were filtering e-mails that went to Mars, one with my name and address would definitely alert them to this message. Chances were, they would let the general's e-mail reach Rawling. And if Rawling replied with the right answer to my question about a dumb joke, I'd know it was him on the other end writing to me. This was the safest way I could think of to reach Rawling, because I still didn't know if the Terratakers had kept control of the dome's mainframe after Dr. Jordan left Mars.

Most important, if the general, who knew I was using his e-mail account, was willing to let Rawling and me correspond, it would tell me I could trust him after all.

And I really needed to be able to do that.

CHAPTER 11

"You want us to what?!" Cannon said through gritted teeth.

I was back inside the room of the jelly cylinders. Ashley stood beside my wheelchair. Nate and Cannon faced us from a few feet away. The hour had passed, and Cannon and Nate were ready to unhook Michael and Joey so Ashley and I could plug in to their robots. And I had just asked my question.

"Yes, sir," I said calmly. "I mean it."

Cannon's square face was red with anger as he strained to keep his voice calm. "You force me to take you to the chopper. You demand to access my personal e-mail but refuse to tell me why. You take your sweet time and make me wait outside the chopper for you like you're the general and I'm some raw recruit. You don't explain a single thing about it on the way back in here. And now you want us to . . . to . . . to . . ."

Cannon lost his voice. He took a big gulp of air and turned to Nate.

Nate shrugged, unsuccessfully trying to hide his smile. "You heard him, General. He wants us to pinch off all the nutrients in the intravenous tubes of the kids on life support."

"Insane!"

"It's not entirely unreasonable," Nate said, letting his smile grow larger. I think Nate liked being out of the army. He didn't have to jump at the general's every command. "As Tyce pointed out, it's only for a few hours. The kids in the jelly cylinders won't be hurt."

"If you think it's so reasonable," Cannon thundered at Nate, "then make your friend here tell us why. All I want to know is why."

Until I received an e-mail from Rawling and I knew Cannon could be trusted, I was going to tell him as little as possible. After all, as far as I knew, Dad was still stuck in that Combat Force prison in the middle of the Everglades. He was depending on me to get him out. To save his life. Even if it took making one of the highest Federation authorities in the country angry at me, I wasn't going to back down.

"You may have noticed," Nate stated, "when you tried to force Tyce to explain earlier with the e-mail stuff, he proved to be very stubborn. I doubt he's changed over the last half hour."

"But pinching off the tubes. How in the world . . . ?" Again, the general's voice failed him.

"It should be simple, sir," I replied. "Fold the tube and tie the fold with a short piece of shoelace. That way all the nutrients will be cut off."

"A short piece of shoelace!" He exploded with so much fury that it surprised me. I was glad I wasn't a raw recruit under his command. "Do you see 23 short pieces of shoelace lying around?"

"Actually, sir," I said quietly, "only 21 pieces. Michael and Joey will be out of the jelly cylinders. Twenty-three minus two leaves—"

"I can do the math!" Cannon paused, and it sounded like he was grinding his teeth. "Do you see 21 pieces of shoelace lying around?"

"Nate has a knife." I'd seen him use it to clean the fish he'd caught for us a few days earlier in the Everglades. That seemed like forever ago.

"A knife!"

"Unless he lost it," I answered.

"And what are we supposed to do with his knife?" Cannon demanded.

I coughed and looked down at the general's feet. He wore high boots, laced tightly.

He followed my gaze. "No! No! No! That's the last straw! Stay behind then. I'll send Ashley by herself."

From my wheelchair, I peered up at Ashley.

She studied me in return, her serious, olive-skinned face

framed by her short dark hair. She lifted her eyes away from mine and faced the general. "I'm with Tyce. We both go, or we both stay."

"Nate!" Cannon pleaded. "Help me out here. They listen to you."

"They're not dumb, General. If Tyce wants the tubes pinched and tied, he's got a good reason for it."

"I just want to know the reason. In any military operation, the commander—"

Nate's smile broadened. "I'm not sure who's the commander anymore." He held up his hand to prevent the general from exploding again. "Remember what these two have survived to get here. You could do worse than listening to them."

Cannon opened his mouth. Then shut it without speaking. He leaned over and began to untie his boots. When he had yanked them off, he straightened up and glared at Nate. "Well," he demanded, standing in his socks, "what's taking you so long?"

"Sir?" Nate said.

"Your stupid knife," Cannon barked. "Where is it? We have some laces to cut."

CHAPTER 12

"Where are you?"

"Here," I answered Ashley through the speakers of my robot. We had both just slipped into robot control, leaving behind the jelly cylinders in Arizona.

"Where is here?" she asked.

"Somewhere in the middle." That was the best answer I could give her. The trailer was filled with robots, and it was totally dark. By the loud hum of wheels against pavement and the rush of wind through the cracks, it was obvious that the trailer was traveling down a highway.

"I'm up near the door," Ashley said.

I reached in front of me. My hand clanked against titanium. How was I going to get there if I couldn't see?

I switched to infrared. My world changed from darkness to a cool blue. We were traveling at night, and a quick temperature reading showed it was in the 40s, which would have been a heat wave on Mars. Like ghosts, the praying mantis shapes of robots—not quite as blue—emerged from the blue of our surroundings. Even though the truck had been traveling for the almost hour that Ashley and I had spent with Nate and Cannon, the robots had not quite cooled down to the temperature of the rest of the inside of the trailer.

"Ashley, I'm on infrared. Wave an arm!"

Her robot did, and I spotted the arm clearly.

"Give me a minute." I lifted the robot in front of me and held it high above my head. Rolling forward to where it had been standing, I spun and set it down where my robot had just stood. I repeated this several more times until my robot finally stood beside Ashley's robot.

"Hello," I said, bowing gravely. My robot head clanked against the door. The back end of my robot, where the battery was a counterweight, bumped into a robot behind me. The clattering seemed deafening, even with the highway noises as a backdrop. "Oops."

Ashley giggled.

Even with all my experience with virtual reality, it was still weird to think that our bodies were actually in blindfolds and headsets in the Arizona desert, while our robots were really only a couple of feet apart. Yet our brain waves sent signals to a computer, which converted them to a digital code and fired them to a satellite that bounced the signals to the receivers on the computers of these robots. Then the robots listened and spoke, and those sound waves were converted into signals bounced back up to the satellite and back down to our bodies, where our brains interpreted them. And all of this back and forth happened at the speed of light—186,000 miles per second—so that our brains responded instantly, as if we were really not controlling our robots but talking person to person.

"Hello," she said. "Since it's hardly been an hour since Dr. Jordan put them to sleep, I'll bet we have plenty of time. Which is good. We've got a lot to talk about. I mean, it's been a long time since we last had a chance to speak without someone else listening."

"Since a Federation ship picked us up from the *Moon Racer* near the moon," I said. About a quarter million miles ago.

"Well . . . ," Ashley began.

"Well, what?" It was difficult enough to read her mind when we faced each other person to person. With robots, it was worse. They weren't capable of facial movements, and with only infrared to guide my vision, it would have been impossible to see her expression clearly anyway.

"What's the deal with all the secret stuff that drove the general crazy?"

"Thanks for backing me," I said. I explained my e-mail and that it seemed safer not to trust the general until we knew for sure he wasn't part of the Terratakers.

"All right," she continued. "I understand why you won't trust the general. Yet. What about cutting off the nutrients of the kids in the jelly cylinders? Aren't they suffering enough?"

"Let me ask you something first. Was Stronsky part of the Institute when you were there?"

"Part of it? When we were young, it was fun. Then a few years ago Stronksy showed up and training got serious. He ruled it like a boot camp."

"What about Dr. Jordan?"

"He stopped by once in a while to watch our progress," Ashley said. "That was it."

"Which makes sense if he had other pods of robot kids to monitor."

Ashley said nothing. The wind and tire-humming noises seemed to grow louder.

"What did I say wrong?" I asked, sensing even in our robot bodies that she was drawing away from me.

"Listen to what you said. 'Pods of robot kids.' Like we're not really human. We are freaks. Not only that, we are freaks created to kill other humans," she said bitterly.

"Not freaks. Not killing by your choice." The only hope I could give her was something I had suggested to Nate just before going out to the helicopter to send my e-mail to Rawling.

"Besides, no one will be killed once Nate and Cannon get to the right people to delay the meeting of the Federation governors. We all agreed that has to be Jordan's target."

"Bad news there," Ashley said after a pause. "While you were in the helicopter, Cannon made a call to the supreme governor to warn him about the soldier robots. The supreme governor told Cannon there was no way he could cancel or postpone the Summit of Governors. He says too many people are waiting for an excuse to say the Federation has no power. He says this is the most important meeting in Federation history. They need a renewed commitment to the Mars Project and to world peace. If people—and the rest of the world's governors—found out that robots spawned by the Mars Project were the threat behind a cancellation of the summit, the Federation might not survive. And the Terratakers would win in the easiest way possible."

I could hardly believe what my robot audio input relayed to my brain. "So it will be better for the world to learn about us after all the governors are killed?"

"The supreme governor told the general there was only one option. That the robots be stopped before the world learns about them. Which is why you and I are here. To find out exactly where these robots are headed."

"But my dad . . . he said we have to expose the robots to the world media and then they'll have to release him from prison."

"Tyce . . ."

By her tone, I knew I wasn't going to like whatever she had to tell me. "Yes?"

"That's the other thing I learned in that call. Your dad is gone from prison."

"Gone! How? Where?"

"The supreme governor didn't say. He just kept repeating that we had to stop Dr. Jordan and keep the world from knowing about the robots."

Dad. Gone. Was he alive? Had someone taken him? I was glad to be controlling this robot body. Unlike mine, its arms and fingers wouldn't shake from fear.

"Don't worry," Ashley said. "Cannon and Nate came up with a solution while you were in the helicopter. They say there has to be a transmitter somewhere nearby that beams all our brain waves by computer code to a satellite. While we're gone, Nate's going to look for it. They figure all they have to do is scramble or stop the transmission, and then all these robots here will be unable to respond to Dr. Jordan's commands."

"What about the death chip?" I asked. "If the robots don't listen, he'll activate it. It would be great if once the transmitter was down, the death chips couldn't be activated, but didn't Joey tell us it's on some highly secret cell-phone frequency?"

"True. But Cannon and Nate believe that Dr. Jordan will first think if the robots don't respond that it's a computer malfunction. They believe that Dr. Jordan will first try to fix the problem. After all—" her voice became sadly bitter—"to Dr. Jordan, we're perfect machines and worth a lot of money. That means we're valuable to him. And he wouldn't want to throw us away that quickly."

"But what if Dr. Jordan doesn't realize it's a malfunction? Or what if he gets mad when the robots don't listen to him? What if he hits the death chip button?"

"Better that the people in the Institute die than 200 world leaders. Better that the kids die than a new world war that might happen if the summit is wrecked." It sounded like Ashley was crying, even though robots can't make tears. "Those were the general's words. Not mine. See? Even to someone who is supposed to be on our side, we're freaks. Disposable machines."

I wanted to be able to comfort her. I searched for words to tell her that she and the other kids were more than just machines. Or freaks. But I couldn't find them. Because deep down—although I had never wanted to admit it to myself— I wondered if she was right.

Freaks. Experiments.

It was true. That's exactly what we were. Ashley, the other kids at the Institute—and me. I'd lived my whole life as a freak because of an experiment gone wrong. I'd never be able to walk like other people could, because Cannon had pushed for funds for a science experiment that would make me a cripple for life. He, Dr. Jordan, and others had used me, just like they'd used the kids in the jelly tubes. Like I was a lab rat. Or a monkey.

It wasn't fair. And I'd have to deal with the unfairness the rest of my life. I wanted to punch a titanium hand against the door of the trailer beside me.

Instead, I forced my mind on what we needed to do next. "Ashley, let's see if we can figure out where the truck is."

"From here?"

"From here. We don't have anything else to do."

At least, I thought, *until the truck stopped.* And then I had no idea what to do after that.

CHAPTER 13

I scanned beyond my immediate surroundings with my infrared, hoping for anything unusual that might give a hint of the truck's location and destination.

The concept of seeing with infrared isn't much different than seeing with light waves. With light waves bringing your brain information, if you were outside on a hill, you could get on your knees and stare at the grass. Your focus range would be a matter of inches. Once you stood, you could change your focus and look a couple of feet away at a butterfly on a flower. Then a couple hundred feet away at a cow in the field. Or a couple of miles across the valley. Or upward at the clouds. Or past the horizon. Your eyes can see from inches away to infinity. Cool, if you think about it.

Same with infrared on that same hillside. You could see

the grass by its contrasting temperature with the ground. The butterfly on the flower would be outlined by its temperature, even if it varied from the air temperature by a tenth of a degree. Same with the cow. And the clouds.

Because there are these similarities, the only difficult part is practice. But after spending enough time in infrared vision, your brain learns to look for patterns, the same way it does with light-based vision.

The biggest difference is what you can and cannot see inside a room. When you rely on light, the walls block you from seeing the light waves on the other side. Not with infrared. Unless the walls are totally insulated, you can still see outlines of things on the other side that are producing more heat than the walls or sucking more cold.

As I scanned, I first looked downward. The exhaust pipe of the truck glowed bright red beneath the cool blue of the trailer floor. The tires directly beneath us, heated by contact with the road, were a blur of orange against the dark, dark blue of the road. At the front, I could make out one human-shaped figure in warm orange on the other side of the trailer wall. By his shape, I guessed him to be Stronsky; Dr. Jordan was too important to stay with the robots.

Looking beyond the sides of the trailer didn't show me much. The night air was a darker blue than the trees, which had soaked up heat during the day. The leaves of the trees

seemed transparent, almost as if I were seeing a color nega-
tive in the light.

Other than that, nothing struck me as unusual.

I wasn't disappointed. I hadn't expected to see much, and
I knew even if somehow I could pinpoint the truck's location
within a couple of miles, it wouldn't help Nate or Cannon. They
had said unless we knew exactly where it was, they wouldn't
be able to set up a roadblock.

I fully expected to have to wait until the truck stopped.

Still, I hated wasting time. Even if I was hoping for
something else to happen right away. After all, the intravenous tubes had been pinched and . . .

"Tyce?" Ashley's voice was soft in my robot audio system.

"Yes, Ashley?"

"Do you think it's easier to believe in God when things
are good in your life? Or when it's bad?"

"What do you mean?"

"Well," she murmured, "I remember all the hours and
hours you and I spent at the telescope under the Mars Dome.
I loved looking out at the universe. It was even fun doing
homework with you. . . . I guess that when you don't have
any major problems and your world is so peaceful, it's easy to
believe God is like a father who loves you."

"Agreed," I said.

On Mars it had seemed natural for Ashley and me to talk
about God. Especially with all of the beauty of the universe

so easy to see and with so much time on Mars to look. Our thoughts wandered to big questions—like how the universe was made, why was it made, and what that meant for a human living in it.

"But," she continued, "it's times like now, when I feel lost and scared and unsure about what's going to happen, that I wonder if God is really there and if he really does love me. I mean, I know that he does in my head, but I just don't *feel* it in my heart."

I thought about it, knowing that she had been taken away from her parents. All she had of her life before the Institute was the pair of silver earrings in the shape of a cross.

"I think," I said, "it's like when I'm with my parents. When I know they're nearby, I don't have much to worry about. And sometimes I don't even think about their presence. I know they'll take care of me. But if I get taken away to someplace strange, like Earth—" I grinned—"then they feel very far away. Because we don't feel as close, it makes me miss them more. So in a way, the times you're lonely and afraid are the times that remind you how much you need God. . . . Make sense?" I asked.

"Makes sense," she whispered.

"If it helps," I said, "right now I feel lost and scared and unsure about what's going to happen next. But I'm glad I'm with you. And that God's watching over us too."

"Me too," she said. "I mean, glad to be with you. Not glad to be with myself."

She giggled, then stopped instantly as a voice spoke from a robot somewhere in the middle of the trailer.

"Hey," the voice said, "is it morning? What's happening? Where am I?"

CHAPTER 14

"Hello," I said, directing my robot voice beyond Ashley's robot. "To answer your questions, it's not morning. You're still in the truck. And we're moving somewhere down a highway."

"Not morning!" This came from another robot at the opposite end of the truck. "Why are we awake?"

Other voices began to join in, and it was difficult to hear what anyone was saying. Then robot arms began to stretch, and robot bodies clanked against each other. Video lenses turned in all directions.

Remember, I was seeing this through infrared. Robots in a lighter blue against a darker blue background. The movement of the skinny stems of the robots and the extended arms and the turning heads looked like a closetful of skeletons coming to life.

"Hello! Hello!" I shouted to get everyone's attention.

That brought relative silence. The wind noise was still loud, and I had to shout to be heard above it.

"Here's what's happened," I said, happy that my guess had been correct. When I wondered about the sleeping drugs that Dr. Jordan used to put the kids to sleep, I realized that he might not want to wake them up at the same time every day. If he administered one big shot when he wanted them to sleep, he'd either have to let it wear off or give them another drug to wake them. It seemed to me it might be simpler if the drugs were put into their bodies on a steady drip that could be shut off automatically on a preset timer in the computer, or manually shut off by instructions to the computer from Dr. Jordan. I began to explain all of this. "Back at the jelly cylinders, your intravenous tubes have been pinched off and—"

"Pinched off! That's the only food we get! We'll starve!"

I could not tell which robot had spoken. "No. There's someone back there to unpinch the tubes. We—"

"Someone's back there? Who? Does Dr. Jordan know?" This from another robot.

"He doesn't know," I said patiently. "That's the whole point of this. So we can talk while he's not watching or listening."

And so that we could talk here through our robot bodies, instead of back at the Institute with the general listening.

"If Dr. Jordan finds out, he'll activate the death chip!"

"We won't let him find out," I answered. "This is our only chance to stop him and—"

"Stop him? Are you crazy? We can't stop him!"

Those words hung in the air. Until someone else asked another question. "Who are you anyway?"

"He's my friend," Ashley said.

"Well, who are you?"

"Ashley, speaking through Number 23."

Immediately buzzing filled the inside of the trailer as all the robots began to speak at once. It only ended when another robot shouted for silence.

"Let me through," the robot insisted when the other voices quieted. "I'll speak for all of us."

There was more clanking and rolling as the robots moved with difficulty. Through the bluish haze, I saw one robot push forward until it reached Ashley's and mine.

"Ashley," the robot said. The voice was not friendly. "This is Kurt speaking. I see you're back."

"Kurt!" Ashley responded. She sounded friendly. A little *too* friendly for my liking. "I missed you! But I couldn't say anything before when Stronsky was around. Let me tell you though, if robots could hug, I'd hug you."

Missed him? Hug? Now I definitely didn't like the friend-liness in her voice.

"I wouldn't let you hug me," Kurt retorted through his

robot. "Not after what you did. Did you get them to fake your death after you escaped?"

"Me?"

"Don't play dumb. What did you two do now—kill Michael and Joey to take their places?"

"What!"

"I guess two more deaths wouldn't matter to you." Kurt sounded bitter. "After all, because of you, half of us got to learn from the other half how the death chips work. And because of you, a bunch of new kids had to replace that first half."

"Half? Killed? Death chips?"

"The half who had agreed with you to try to escape. Stronsky told us what you did. Gave him their names so you could be set free and leave the rest of us behind. But he told us you'd been killed too, which made us all very happy."

"What!" Ashley sounded like she was in shock. "That's not true. I had no choice. Dr. Jordan took me away."

"More like he brought you back to spy on us again," Kurt threw back.

"No! Dr. Jordan took me to the Mars Dome. He—"

"Mars," Kurt interrupted. I heard a sneer in his voice. "*Right.* Most of Earth knows the *truth* about the Mars Dome."

Much as I wanted to punch this robot with my own titanium fists, I simply asked, "Which is?"

"There's no Mars Dome. It's all a fake. Every time the Federation wants to keep people happy about sucking the world's resources, they bring out new footage showing progress on Mars. But we all know it's some computer-generated images that any Hollywood producer could put together."

"I see," I said.

"You do?" Again, I sensed the sneer that could not be hidden through a robot's speakers. "And who exactly are you? I mean, being Ashley's friend isn't a good thing."

"Me? I was the first kid born on Mars."

Kurt laughed, and other robot laughter grew behind him.

Although I knew better—that one robot punching another would not prove much—emotion won. I raised my fist.

Ashley stepped between us. "Listen," she insisted, "there will be time to sort this out later. And when we're done, you'll see that Tyce and I are telling the truth. For now, though, we have to work together."

"Why?" Kurt asked loudly. "Even if we could trust you, why should we risk our lives and work against Dr. Jordan and Stronsky? You heard what he said today about our parents."

"Whenever this truck gets to where it is going," I said, "they are going to use us as an army."

"We know that." The sneer again. "It's just some more training. In some sort of virtual-reality war game."

"Not a game," I said. "You'll be shooting real people. The governors of every country of the world. Dr. Jordan wants us to destroy their summit meeting and start a new world war."

"Ha-ha," Kurt said. "You and Ashley make quite a pair.

First you've been to Mars, and now we're going to start a world war."

"Maybe we should listen to them," a voice in the back said.

"Really," Kurt said sarcastically. "So Dr. Jordan can get a new list of the rebels among us? So he'll activate a bunch more death chips? So our parents will be killed?"

I jumped in because I didn't want to allow anyone to answer. "We can prove we're telling the truth."

In the blue haze, robot heads swiveled my way.

"Why don't a few of you jump out of robot control and go back?"

"Back?" came a voice. This one sounded afraid. "I'd rather be asleep than wake up back in the jelly cylinder. I can't see or hear, and my body feels so trapped."

"What's your answer to *that*?" Kurt said.

"Simple. Those of you who go back just call out for help. General Cannon and a guy named Nate will help you take off the wax over your eyes and ears so you can see and hear. Then you'll see Michael and Joey. You'll know they're alive. And the general and Nate will tell you why we need to stop Dr. Jordan."

"Fine then," Kurt said. "We'll do that." He spoke to everyone else. "I need three volunteers."

He got them.

It took less than a minute for all three to return to controlling their robots.

"Kurt," the first one said, "these two are lying to us."

CHAPTER 15

"Lying?" I raised my robot arms in protest. "Impossible."

"No one came," the first kid said. "I screamed for help. No one came. It was horrible, feeling my body stuck there. Like a spider had me all wrapped up. I was blind and deaf. Finally I came back here. At least when I control my robot, my brain doesn't feel like it's stuck in a black box."

The other robot voices began to babble again.

"Silence!" Kurt shouted.

As the truck roared down the highway, the voices died down.

"Do you other two agree?"

They both said yes. No one had helped them.

"And that from three of us who have no reason to lie," Kurt put in. "Because if there was a chance to be rescued, we would take it. Three of us against two of them. We know Ashley already turned traitor against us. And a friend of hers is probably an enemy of ours."

I could hardly believe this. We were their only hope, and yet there was nothing Ashley and I could do to get them to believe us.

"I would say," Kurt continued, "that it's obvious what we should do."

"No," Ashley protested. "Listen to me. I was sent to Mars. I was supposed to test a space torpedo called the Hammerhead. But it was intended to kill millions of people. So instead I crashed it into one of the moons of Mars. Then Tyce came back with me to help find you guys. Dr. Jordan, who was in a prison on the ship, took over the computer and escaped in a pod. He had programmed the spaceship to crash into the sun, but we . . ." Her voice trailed off as she realized how crazy it must sound to the other kids.

"Ha-ha," Kurt answered. "This isn't story time, you know. And we're not stupid." Then he spoke to the other robots. "You know what Stronsky promised when we began training in these war games. Once we prove ourselves to Dr. Jordan, he's going to let us show the entire world what we can do. Then people will know that armies like ours can protect them. We'll be heroes."

Some of the kids cheered at this.

Kurt paused. "Not only will we be heroes, we'll still be

alive. Which definitely won't happen if we follow these two against Dr. Jordan."

"You're wrong," I said. I raised my voice to the others. "The only way you can stay alive is by defeating Dr. Jordan."

Voices began to chatter again.

"Everyone!" Kurt shouted. "Listen!"

They listened.

"You know they're lying to us," he said. "I say we tear their bot-packs off so they can't try anything here. In the morning Dr. Jordan can activate their death chips. That will catch up with them, no matter how far they run in their real bodies."

Our death chips?

Ashley spoke my thoughts. "Kurt, I wasn't around when you were put in the jelly cylinders. The death chips don't scare me."

Kurt laughed. "You weren't around because you turned traitor. But you also missed hearing everything they told us about the death chips, didn't you?"

Ashley's silence told him enough.

"See," he taunted, "the same satellite that beams our signals to the robots will also beam an activation signal anytime Stronsky or Jordan want. Just like a GPS, the signal will track you down. Then *poof*! You're dead."

"Not me," Ashley said, with a little less certainty than before.

"Of course you. We found out they didn't implant the death chips when they put us in the jelly cylinders. No, they did it when they operated on us for the spinal plugs. All those years we never knew that little bomb was waiting inside us. Not until we watched half of us die. The half that you betrayed.

"Yes, Ashley. We saw Stronsky push the button, and they died—in front of us. Just slowly fell and then stopped moving. In the morning, the same will happen to you. Justice will be served."

"Please," I said intensely. "Listen to Ashley. She's telling you the truth. She didn't betray any of you."

"Then how did Stronsky know the ones who were planning to try to escape?"

I had no answer for that. Neither did Ashley. But we knew the story couldn't be true.

"Then consider yourselves guilty," Kurt insisted. "Okay, everyone. Time to vote. Here's the plan of action. We tear the bot-packs off their robot bodies and disable them. In the morning, we report this to Dr. Jordan and let him activate the death chip. How many yes votes?"

In the hazy blue, there was no movement behind him. Not at first. Then one hand went up. And another two. Another three.

It didn't take a genius to figure out where this was headed. If we were still connected when the bot-packs were torn off our bodies, it could blow our own brain circuits. Sudden disconnection was far worse than any shock.

"Ashley," I said urgently, "we'd better go."

Without waiting for her to say anything, I shouted *Stop!* in my mind to release myself from robot control.

And fell into darkness.

CHAPTER 16

Back in the jelly cylinder room, I shouted as I tore at my blindfold and headset. "Ashley! Ashley!"

Finally clear of my blindfold, I saw her sitting against the wall, motionless.

Nate and Cannon were gone. So were Michael and Joey.

"Ashley!" I began to wheel toward her. "Ashley!"

I knew she couldn't hear me, not with her ears covered, but that didn't stop me from shouting again. "Ashley!"

Then I saw her hands move, and I let out a deep sigh of relief.

As I reached her, she was taking off her own blindfold. She blinked her eyes a couple of times in order to focus on this room. And then she smiled.

"Ashley."

"I'm back," she said. "Where are the others?"

"Not sure. But it explains why the three kids who returned didn't get any help." I pointed at the jelly cylinders where the intravenous tubes were pinched and tied with pieces of shoelace. "We've got to untie those tubes and get them all back to sleep again. And then figure something out in the remaining hours until Dr. Jordan wakes them up."

The other four returned about 10 minutes later, with Michael and Joey trailing the big men.

"You're back," Cannon said. "I thought we agreed you were going to stay with all the other robots and try to find out what was planned next."

Ashley quickly filled them in.

"Let me get this straight," he said when she finished. "The truck is going to arrive at its destination, and you won't be able to get back into your robots because they were disconnected."

"Yes, sir," I answered for her. "I doubt we put them to sleep fast enough to prevent them from disconnecting the robot computers."

"And as soon as Dr. Jordan wakes them up and talks to them, he'll learn about you two. And he'll . . ." I could tell the general's mind was racing ahead.

"Yes, sir. If the death chip works like he says, Ashley's chip will be activated."

"Michael." The general turned to him. "Was everything Kurt told these two correct? Half of your group?"

"Right in front of us," Michael said, shivering. "Stronsky showed us his little remote. He let us watch him push the button. They all slowly fell down. And then some of the aides dragged them away. The next morning a bunch of younger kids were brought in to replace them. In the afternoon they put us in the jelly cylinders."

The general frowned. He turned his gaze back to me. "Why only Ashley's death chip? Why not yours?"

Mine? "Sir, I wasn't part of this group of kids. My operation took place on Mars."

"What makes you assume Dr. Jordan doesn't have a death chip implanted in you, too?"

"I . . . I . . ." I couldn't come up with an answer. Horror filled me as I understood. If the death chip were part of the operation, why wouldn't it have been done to me, too?

When the truck arrived at its destination, and as soon as Dr. Jordan woke up the robots and found out that Ashley and I had survived, he would press a little button and send a signal that would stop our hearts.

Cannon closed his eyes, then opened them again. He spoke very quietly. "This changes things, doesn't it?"

CHAPTER 17

I was back in the helicopter again at my unfolded comp-
board, with my system just booted. Yes, we were running out
of time, and Ashley and I should have been doing something
else. But what? Cannon, Nate, Joey, Michael, Ashley, and
I had spent the last 45 minutes trying to come up with a
solution.

And we couldn't decide on anything.

I desperately wanted some good news.

Like the fact that Rawling had read my e-mail and been
able to reply.

My comp-board had finally loaded and connected to the
Internet. I stared glumly at my computer screen as I accessed
Cannon's e-mail account.

Then I smiled as I read the first and only message. With all that had gone wrong, I at least knew now that I could trust Cannon.

From: "Rawling McTigre" <mctigrer@marsdome.ss>
To: "General Jeb McNamee" <mcnameej@combatforce.gov>
Sent: 03.31.2040, 12:05 a.m.
Subject: Re: Please read this right away!

Tyce,

When you banged your robot head during that expedition, I said it was as hard as your own stubborn skull and that you were so used to banging it against things that you no longer needed any pills for a headache.

Yes, it's me. And I'm so relieved to hear from you. The real you.

Yes, I had been getting responses to the e-mails I'd been sending you, but they were strange responses and I was beginning to wonder if it really was you. In fact, during the last week I had a trusted computer programmer go through the mainframe, and he found the secret programming that allowed someone in the dome to intercept all the messages. It's a long story—one that I want to tell you when you get back—but right now I'm playing cat and mouse, sending real e-mails with one program and fake e-mails with the other program. I'm hoping to find out who here on Mars is secretly logging on to the mainframe.

In short, you can trust this message. I wish I could do more than this though. Your e-mail brought up too many disturbing questions, and I'm 50 million miles away.

By the urgency of your message, I hope and expect you will check your e-mail soon. I've dropped everything here and am waiting in front of my computer screen for your reply to this. (I've printed out your Moon Racer journal and will read it as I wait so that I'll be as up-to-date as possible.)

I know there is a time lag, but as soon as I get your next e-mail, I'll send you one back. It will be the closest thing we can have to a live conversation.

And, Tyce? I'll be praying too.

Your friend,

Rawling

P.S. I don't want to say anything to your mother until I know as much as possible. I'm worried enough. She'll go through the roof of the dome unless I can answer all her questions.

It gave me strength to know that Rawling was waiting. So I began to type.

From: "General Jeb McNamee"
<mcnameej@combatforce.gov>
To: "Rawling McTigre" <mctigrer@marsdome.ss>
Sent: 03.31.2040, 12:26 a.m.
Subject: Got it

Rawling! Thanks! Just sending this to let you know I've read
your e-mail. During the lag for this to reach you and your
next message to reach me, I'll put together a longer one
with more details and send it ASAP.
   Your friend,
   Tyce

I hit send. Then I immediately began to explain all that
I could in a longer e-mail. I knew I had about 20 minutes
before I heard back from Rawling.

There wasn't much good news. Actually, there wasn't
any good news. Starting with the fact that my dad had disappeared from prison, and that now, even if we stopped Dr.
Jordan, I wouldn't know how to find Dad.

Here, Cannon and Nate had gone searching for the
transmitter with Michael and Joey. That's why they were
gone when the three kids tried to verify Ashley's story. The
bad news was that they hadn't been able to find the transmitter in the darkness.

Nate had suggested that since Ashley and I could no longer secretly work among the robot soldiers, we should just unplug all the kids from their jelly cylinders. That way none of the robots would be operational, and Dr. Jordan wouldn't hear about Ashley and me from any of the other kids.

Cannon then told us he was about to make the most difficult decision he'd ever made as a general. That he couldn't do that, even if it would save our lives. Then he explained why.

Since they couldn't find the transmitter here on the mountain, he would have to call in for Combat Force surveillance to use three of their satellites to triangulate the signals from here to Dr. Jordan's receiving satellite. Because this required three Combat Force satellites, it would take hours for all of them to be in the required positions. Then, once they were in position, we'd need exactly 20 minutes to triangulate the location.

When I asked why Dr. Jordan's satellite was so important, Cannon said there were thousands of satellites in orbit. They'd have to find it first. Once they did, they could pull it in and find out where it had been sending and receiving other signals, because that would allow the Combat Force to find all the other pods of kids.

Timing was crucial then. I pointed out that Dr. Jordan might move the army so quickly that the robot soldiers would be in position to kill immediately. Cannon's solution was to have someone call him at the first sign of trouble, at which he would unplug the kids here and shut down their robot control. That was not good. Being shocked into disconnection was bad enough. But to be unplugged without warning . . .

It meant that in worst-case scenario some of the kids would die, and most of them would suffer brain damage. The time to unplug them was *before* they went into control mode. Once their brains were actively engaged with the robot computer, any short circuit or disconnection caused brutal damage.

Just as I finished putting all of this into my e-mail, my computer chirped, telling me I had mail. I held off on sending my message and opened and scanned what Rawling had sent me.

From: "Rawling McTigre" <mctigrer@marsdome.ss>
To: "General Jeb McNamee" <mcnameej@combatforce.gov>
Sent: 03.31.2040, 12:55 a.m.
Subject: Waiting at my computer

All right, Tyce, send me what you have. Hopefully I won't have many questions, and hopefully I can answer any questions you have for me.
    Rawling

Questions for him? Sure. Like how Ashley and I might stop Dr. Jordan from activating our death chips. Or how

Cannon might stop Jordan after he had killed us by activating our death chips. I didn't word it exactly like that, but I hoped I got the message across. I just finished my e-mail by asking Rawling to offer any suggestions, and most of all, to continue to pray for us. I also sent a hug through him to my mom. I knew she'd be terribly worried once she found out about this.

I sent this message and began my wait again. As the minutes ticked by with incredible slowness, I decided to write another e-mail. This one to my mother. To tell her how much I loved her and how much she meant to me.

I held off on sending the e-mail, though, because I knew it would make her too sad.

Somewhere inside me, I still had a little hope. Maybe Rawling would think of something we had missed.

His next message arrived exactly 20 minutes later.

From: "Rawling McTigre" <mctigrer@marsdome.ss>
To: "General Jeb McNamee" <mcnameej@combatforce.gov>
Sent: 03.31.2040, 1:15 a.m.
Subject: Re: The whole story

Tyce,
I've received your e-mail. Hang tight on your end while I think things through.
Rawling

I hung tight. And exactly one hour later, his next e-mail arrived. It showed that, yes, Rawling *had* thought things through.

I called for Grunt, the helicopter pilot, to help me down to the ground and into my wheelchair.

And I rolled as fast as I could back toward the jelly cylinders.

CHAPTER 18

"Ugly and weird. We drove 36 hours to deliver these?"

We were glad for that 36 hours. Without that one extra day of travel, Ashley and I would probably be so sleep deprived we'd never have a chance to succeed.

After getting that e-mail from Rawling, it had been a lot easier to return from the helicopter to the general. Cannon could be trusted. So I'd told him everything.

We'd come up with a plan.

Then we'd slept, since Cannon insisted rested soldiers were effective soldiers.

After waking, almost at noon the next day, all of us had waited in suspense as Cannon had found some trusted people in the military to begin a search for the moving truck. It was a next-to-impossible chance to find it but worth trying, because then we could stop the robot soldiers with no risk.

Instead, the hours had dragged on while we got everything ready that we could. Then Cannon had insisted that Ashley and I sleep again. He'd woken us up at midnight, and she and I had been controlling the robot bodies in the trailer ever since.

Just waiting for the truck to stop.

Which was now.

The truck driver had opened the door to the trailer. He spoke to his assistant, who stood beside him. They looked similar. Shaved heads, skinny, in leather jackets and blue jeans. Both puffed on cigarettes as they surveyed the robots. Including the new ones that Ashley and I now controlled.

"No wonder that muscle freak left us alone to do this," his helper agreed. They stood on a warehouse dock. Nothing in the background gave any clues as to where we had stopped after hours in the trailer among the motionless robots. "These are really, really ugly. Really, really weird. Like a bunch of stick insects I seen on the Nature Channel accidentally one night when I was looking for music videos. What do you call them? Paving mantras?"

The first part of our plan had been the simplest. Since robots 17 and 23 had disconnected computers, Cannon and Nate had helped two other kids out of jelly cylinders and Ashley and I had replaced them. I was now Number 9, and

Ashley was 16. Back in the desert mountains, those kids were out of their jelly cylinders and happy to be moving around normally.

"Paving Mantras?" the driver said. "I ain't heard of that rock band."

"Not a rock band. That's the name of those stick insects. Paving mantras."

"*Paying* mantras is more like it," the driver said, flicking ashes. "We've never made easier money. Keys were in the truck like the guy on the phone said. Map was waiting. And for a change, New York traffic wasn't bad."

"You've never been up before 10 in the morning," the second guy said. "Of course you wouldn't know what the streets are like this early."

The first man sucked hard on his cigarette and grinned. "Still haven't been up before 10 in the morning."

"Huh?"

"Haven't gone to sleep yet. But as soon as we unload these creepy things, I'm gonna spend a wad of money on a fancy hotel room and sleep and sleep. Driving all night ain't my idea of a good time. I'm gonna get up only to order room service and fill my face. How does that sound?"

"Me," the second guy put in, "I've got a list of horses that can't lose. I'm taking my money and tripling it at the racetracks."

"Yeah, yeah. Got those directions that were under the

mat? Remember, the guy said the money would be waiting for us in the storage room where we deliver these."

"I got the directions. You got the keys and passwords to get into this building?"

"Yup. Good thing," the first guy said. He threw his cigarette down. "You know them governors are meeting at some kind of summit around here. I don't think you could get into any of these buildings without a password for the security pads."

"Yeah. That voice on the phone must be well connected."

"He's got money. You got money, you got connections."

It was the second guy's turn to grin. "I guess then you and me have now got connections."

One by one they began to lift out the robots in front of Ashley and me. I noticed that 17 and 23 had loose wires dangling where the bot-packs had been ripped away. Neither the driver nor his assistant noticed, however. They treated those two robots like the others. Once on the dock they rolled each one out of sight. I couldn't see where they went, but they weren't gone long between each robot, and Ashley and I didn't dare speak to each other.

The trailer was empty of robots before they reached ours.

"What do you think these things do?" the second guy asked, picking up the robot that Ashley controlled.

The first guy shrugged. "Got to be for some kind of

science-fiction movie. You know, just another story where something attacks someone in New York City."

"Yeah, yeah. Someone in movies has the kind of money to call us up and tell us where to find this truck. I mean, all of it was right there like he promised."

The first guy leaned forward to pick up my robot. His face was so close to my video lens that I could see his blackheads oozing out of his pores. Cradling my robot in his arms, he walked onto the dock, into the building, and then pushed the robot forward down the hallway. He reached the storage room as his assistant was stepping out. They squeezed by each other.

Even with all the sleep that the general had insisted we get, the stress of suspense had made me feel a little goofy. At least that's my only explanation for what I did next, without even thinking about it. With my hand low and out of sight, I pinched the assistant's leg as we passed him in the doorway.

"Hey! Why'd you do that?"

"Do what?" the driver said, pushing my robot among the others and turning to face his assistant.

"Don't mess with me, man. Were you trying to take the money out of my pocket?"

"Me?"

"Like who else grabbed me?"

"You saying I grabbed you?"

The door to the storage room slammed shut. Their voices disappeared gradually as they continued to argue.

In the dimness of the storage room, Ashley giggled. "I saw what you did. I just wish you could have seen the look on the guy's face."

I laughed with her, but neither of us laughed for long.

We knew what was ahead.

CHAPTER 19

I could not guess how much time had passed since all the robots had been unloaded into this large storage room. But each second seemed like a year. Ashley and I didn't talk—we didn't know when one of the robots around us might wake. And we didn't know when Dr. Jordan or Stronsky or both of them would open the storage room door. It was too important now that our identity among the other robots remain a secret.

As we waited, my mind kept going in circles. About the only question that had been answered by the two deliverymen was our approximate location. Our robot bodies were in downtown New York City near the summit meeting. Which meant the targets were definitely the governors of the Federation.

But how did Dr. Jordan intend to get us into the room?

More importantly, when?

The best case would be as late as possible. The brain-wave activity that Ashley and I were sending to these robots was enough transmission for the Combat Force satellites to get the location of Dr. Jordan's receiving satellite. Those three satellites would be in the right positions to triangulate at 7:00 a.m. Arizona time—9:00 a.m. New York time. And it would take 20 minutes for the triangulation. If Dr. Jordan didn't intend to attack until after that, Cannon and Nate would be able to get Dr. Jordan's satellite position, then unplug all the other kids before they were hooked up through virtual reality, so every robot in this room would be useless. That would leave me and Ashley to face Dr. Jordan and Stronsky as they opened the door.

But if Dr. Jordan's attack was planned before 9:20 . . .

That's what made waiting so difficult. Thinking about the worst-case scenario.

Cannon would wait as long as possible to unplug the kids, hoping for enough time to triangulate. But he was on a direct cell-phone line to someone he'd sent to join the governors. If these robots somehow managed to breach security and reach the summit, he'd have to pull the plug on each of the kids in the jelly tubes except for me and Ashley. And because they'd be actively connected to the robots through virtual reality, their brains would never be the same.

And Ashley and I would remain in robot control, because if everyone else was unplugged, it was crucial for Ashley and me to continue our brain-wave transmissions for the triangulation efforts.

Worst of all, we'd have to face Dr. Jordan and his death chip activator.

I sure hoped Rawling's theories were right.

I let these thoughts circle through my mind until finally, finally, I heard the sound of robots waking up around me.

Shortly after that, the storage room door opened.

Dr. Jordan and Stronsky stood framed against the light.

"Good morning, boys and girls," Dr. Jordan said. "Are we all awake and ready for a big day?"

"Last night we had to disconnect the computers to Numbers 17 and 23," Kurt reported. His robot stood in the hallway, alone with Dr. Jordan and Stronsky. Barely 30 seconds after the door opened, Kurt had raised his robot arm to tattle on us.

"Numbers 17 and 23," Stronsky repeated.

I was listening to them because I had amplified my hearing. Trouble was, to get their words, the background noise had to be a lot higher too. I could also hear the scratching of cockroaches in the nearby walls, a sound I'd learned, to my disgust, during my time in the Florida prison. "I'm not surprised. Those two gave me trouble during yesterday's training session."

"Shut up, idiot," Dr. Jordan hissed. "Don't you understand? If this happened last night, that means the kids weren't asleep."

His tone changed as he directed his next words to Kurt's robot. "Isn't that right, Number 19?"

"Yes, sir. It was the weirdest thing. Just like that, I popped awake. So I started robot control, expecting to see you. But we were in the back of the trailer. Everyone else woke up, and Ashley started to tell us—"

"Ashley!" Dr. Jordan interrupted Kurt with fierceness that would have scared a bear protecting her cubs.

"Yes, Ashley. I mean, I know you sent her there to test us to see who would rebel against you. I thought it would be better to make her quiet so that the younger kids wouldn't be tempted to do something stupid. I mean, you asked me to protect them by reporting everything to you."

There was a long pause. "You did send her, didn't you?" Kurt asked, his uncertainty amplified 100 times in my robot hearing.

I could guess what Kurt was suddenly thinking. Because if Dr. Jordan had not sent Ashley, then it meant Ashley had been telling the truth. She wasn't a traitor to the rest of the kids.

"Of course I sent her," Dr. Jordan said after the briefest of pauses.

"That's what I thought, sir." Kurt sounded relieved. If my robot had had teeth, I'd have been grinding them at how badly Kurt was trying to be a teacher's pet. "I have to admit, that Tyce person sounded like the real thing for a second or two. His story about being from Mars fit exactly with what she was telling us."

Dr. Jordan sucked in a breath. Now I could imagine what he was thinking. That I was supposed to be dead. "Yes, Tyce. So you disconnected their robot computers? Did anything else happen?"

"No, sir. I might have dozed off. Next thing I knew we were all here in this storage room."

"Thank you, Number 19."

"I just thought of something," Kurt added. "You're not going to activate the death chip on them, are you? I mean, if they're secretly working for you . . ."

"Of course not." I wondered if Dr. Jordan simply meant not while Kurt was watching. Because then Kurt would realize that Ashley and I were enemies of Dr. Jordan.

I heard Kurt's robot wheels squeak against the floor as he turned away. Then another squeak. He'd pivoted back to Dr. Jordan.

"You will remember all my help, won't you?" Kurt asked. "After this is over, you will free me from the cylinder like you promised?"

"Of course," Dr. Jordan said smoothly. "Just remember to do your best in this next mission. We're almost ready to begin."

Kurt rolled back to join us.

Dr. Jordan remained in the hallway. He didn't talk to

Stronsky. Probably because he was thinking through what he had just learned from Kurt. Among his lies to Kurt was the one that meant the most to Ashley and me.

The one where he had promised Kurt that he wouldn't activate our death chips.

I knew that was a lie for three reasons. One, since he knew that Ashley and I had taken control of a couple of robots here, he also knew that she and I were back at the Institute, thousands of miles away, where the only way he could stop us quickly was by killing us.

Two, he knew from Kurt that Ashley and I had spent part of last night trying to convince all the other kids to help us. Which meant to him that if Ashley and I were still alive and back at the Institute, we would be doing our best to stop him.

And three, he had already tried to kill us a couple of times by other means.

So I waited, wondering what would happen to the heart in my body back at the Institute. Wondering if blinding pain would take me away from robot control. Wondering if I would die in the next 30 seconds.

CHAPTER 20

I did not die in the next 30 seconds. Or the next minute.

Which meant Rawling had guessed right. The first part of his last e-mail to me had been very simple:

Tyce,

I doubt Dr. Jordan would kill the kids in the jelly tubes. He has invested too much time and money in their operations and training. My guess is he wanted to replace some of the older kids with younger ones and ship the older kids somewhere else, so he made it look like he had killed them. It would be easy. Slip some sort of knockout capsule in their food and activate it with everyone watching. Pretend to make them an example and tell everyone that Ashley had betrayed them. I know it will be gambling with your life, but if *he really has the power to activate the death chip, you have nothing to lose. I think it's a bluff. There's no such thing as a death chip. Why? Because if Dr. Jordan had really implanted a death chip in you and Ashley, he'd have activated it a long time ago the other times he had tried killing you. I'm sure he is very, very annoyed that he hasn't gotten rid of you yet!*

Inside the storage shed, I slowly moved the robot head to look over at the robot that Ashley controlled. She, in turn, had swiveled its head to look at my robot. She nodded slightly. I did the same to her.

We were still alive!

Dr. Jordan stepped into the doorway again to address us. Stronsky was nowhere to be seen.

Now came the difficult part.

Dr. Jordan checked his watch. "In 15 minutes, your targets will be assembled. At that time the computer will arm your lasers. Five minutes after that, you will complete your mission."

He surveyed the robots. "Your task today will be no different than the way you have trained for this mission. Number 19 will lead you. He will throw a smoke bomb immediately upon entering the room. Switch to infrared and destroy the targets. Thus, in 20 minutes, I want all of them dead."

"Dead?" This came from robot 9. "This is a virtual-reality mission, right? To prove we can be great soldiers."

"Yes, yes," Dr. Jordan said in a soothing voice. He glanced at his watch again. "None of you need to worry about a thing."

"But it seems you've gone to a lot of trouble and—"

Dr. Jordan interrupted by pulling a small remote from his pocket and aiming it at Number 9. "Let's see," he said, staring down at the remote. "I punch in 9 and . . ."

"No!" the kid controlling the robot yelled. "I believe you."

I desperately wanted to tell the kids it was a bluff. That Rawling had been right. There was no death chip. But if I did that and Dr. Jordan thought he was on the verge of losing control, he himself might use his remote control to shut down the transmission from the satellite. And we still needed time to triangulate. It wouldn't happen without a continuous stream of digital signals bouncing back and forth.

"Let me remind all of you," Dr. Jordan threatened. "If just one of you disobeys or tries to stop this mission, I will activate the death chip in the heart of every single person here." He looked carefully at each of the robots. "There are two of you here who know what I mean."

So he'd guessed that Ashley and I had returned by using different robots!

But he hadn't guessed we knew he was only bluffing about the death chip. So that meant we had a better shot at stopping him from killing the governors at the summit. But would we be able to get the triangulation signal before

Cannon unplugged all the kids in their jelly cylinders? If that happened, it would be just like activating a death chip, because some of the kids might die.

"Two of us here know what you mean?" Kurt repeated.

"Oh, shut your whining mouth," Dr. Jordan snapped. "We're down to 17 minutes. Follow me to the street. Stronsky will take over from there."

CHAPTER 21

Twenty-one of us rolled our robots as we followed Stronsky down the sidewalk, with hundreds of passersby barely glancing at us. So this was what the truck driver and his assistant had meant about New York. Nothing was new, and nobody was impressed at anything. We could have been invisible, for all the city's reaction to 21 robots rolling in single file.

I glanced around. A bright sun beamed down from a beautiful blue sky. I was hardly used to seeing blue sky as it was—on Mars the sky is butterscotch colored—and I realized I hadn't seen much light at all in the last couple of days. Plus, my thoughts had been so filled with stress, it just seemed like the world was dark.

I'd forgotten how amazing a blue sky could look.

And, since I'd never been in a big city before, I was also

amazed at the buildings and vehicles and the sheer number of people who ignored us as they flowed around the robots.

The noise was nearly overwhelming. Horns, shouting, sirens.

This was New York City!

I wished badly I could just be a tourist. Not a freak controlling a robot because someone had operated on me when I was little.

But I had to worry about time.

We approached a large public square surrounded by grand buildings, and on one of them, a large clock plainly showed the time. I checked it against my hidden countdown device.

Twelve minutes past nine. The triangulation had begun 12 minutes ago! The three Federation satellites in three different orbits were tracking the transmission beams that came from the mountaintop in Arizona. As soon as they'd been able to gather enough data, they could fire a laser at Dr. Jordan's satellite and knock it out of orbit. All transmissions to these robots would end.

Twelve minutes past nine.

Eight minutes to go.

And what looked like now only five minutes until we reached the building where the Summit of Governors met.

Was there a way Ashley or I could slow down this procession?

As we neared the largest building five minutes later, I relaxed. Twenty armed Federation soldiers guarded the entrance. They wouldn't let us in without a fight. Surely that would take more than a couple of minutes.

That's all we needed. A delay.

Except as we rolled up the wheelchair ramp to the wide doors of the main entrance, the soldiers stepped aside.

One of them saluted Stronsky.

All of the soldiers were on the side of the Terratakers!

We entered with no delay.

Now three minutes and counting . . .

I looked around for Dr. Jordan. That had been the next part of the plan: to take him hostage as we approached the summit. That way he'd be prisoner, and we could hold him long enough for the triangulation to finish.

No Dr. Jordan.

Instead, the robots continued to roll down a wide hallway, with a nice carpet that hushed the sound of our wheels.

Where was Dr. Jordan?!

At the end of the long hallway four more Federation soldiers guarded another gleaming door.

We'd get there in less than a minute. But my countdown device showed we needed at least two more minutes for successful triangulation and to disable the satellite. Two minutes. Which we desperately needed. If those soldiers ahead let us through as well, one of two things would happen. The robots would kill the governors. Or back in the desert, Cannon would be forced to unplug the kids in the cylinders while they were still connected, killing or brain-damaging them.

Where was Dr. Jordan?!

All right then, I told myself. *Take Stronksy.*

I sped up the rolling of my wheels and reached him. Grabbing his arm, I spun him toward me.

"What?" he snarled. Few men were bigger than he was, and even fewer carried more muscle bulk. Yet he couldn't shake off my robot's grasp. The machine in my control was five times more powerful than the world's best human soldiers. "Let go!"

"No. Stop all these robots."

"Have you lost your mind!" he exclaimed. "You want Dr. Jordan activating all the death chips?"

"We both know there are no death chips. Now give the order to stop!" I put my other hand around his throat and applied pressure. "You know the strength these robots have, Stronsky. Your neck will be skinnier than a pencil when I finish squeezing."

"Tyce, I wondered when you would try your usual cheese-ball heroics. Only this time it won't work." Dr. Jordan's voice came from a miniature walkie-talkie on a string around Stronsky's massive neck. "Surprised to hear from me? Did you really think I wouldn't find a way to monitor this?"

"Stop the kids," I said. I squeezed harder and Stronsky

grunted. "Or I activate Stronsky's death chip the old-fashioned way."

"I highly doubt that, Tyce. You haven't got the guts to kill him. Besides, even if you did, you wouldn't be able to stop the robots. They don't trust you, and you don't have enough time to explain." Dr. Jordan stopped, then addressed Stronsky. "Are you near the summit doors?"

"Ten yards," he grunted.

"Good. Proceed as planned."

Even though I had Stronsky by the neck, he waved all the robots forward.

CHAPTER 22

"Stop!" I had to delay them just one more minute.

"Stop?" The squealing protest came from, of course, Kurt, who was running Number 19. "Are you trying to get all of us killed?"

"No, I—"

The robots kept rolling forward.

"Really," Ashley pleaded. "Stop! You don't have to kill anyone!"

None of the robots slowed down.

This was too crazy. We'd actually found a way to stop Dr. Jordan and rescue the kids from the jelly cylinders, but they wouldn't listen. They didn't believe us. And because of it, they were less than a minute away from being unplugged from their robots. It seemed like there was nothing we could do to save them.

The soldiers ahead stepped aside. One of them began to open the door. They too were Terratakers who had infiltrated the Federation army!

A deep voice reached us. I recognized it. It belonged to the old man I'd met in prison. The man my father had been holding at knifepoint in the cell. The man I'd found out later was the supreme governor, with the most political power in the world. From where I was in the hallway, I could see his distinguished features at a podium as he spoke into a microphone.

No! I wanted to shout in frustration. In 30 more seconds, the triangulation would be complete, the transmitting satellite disabled. But Kurt was almost through the doorway, ready to toss the smoke bomb that would lead to the deaths of all these governors. We wouldn't get those seconds!

"Aaaaagh!"

In my panic, I'd forgotten I was still clutching Stronsky by the neck. As my frustration and panic grew, I'd accidentally begun to squeeze harder.

I dropped him. He fell like a sack of dirt.

"You'll never stop us," he said. "No matter how badly you might defeat us here."

I wasn't worried at this point about the long-term defeat of the Terratakers. Just about saving the lives of the governors in the room beyond.

I scanned the hallway, desperate for something, anything, that might delay us.

Two things grabbed my attention.

One I was familiar with.

The other I only knew because of what I was able to read in white letters against a red background. It was a lever. And the instructions plainly told me to: Pull in case of fire.

Kurt was a few feet from the door. He lifted his robot arm to toss the smoke bomb. When the supreme governor saw the motion, he stopped speaking.

Once Cannon's observer in the room noticed the robot at the door, Cannon would begin unplugging them!

I was down to less than 10 seconds. Spinning over to the side of the wall, I pulled as instructed.

Immediately a loud clanging echoed through the building. So loud I could barely hear Ashley. That was good. It meant that anyone trying to get a message to Cannon wouldn't be heard either.

But it was also bad. Because if Cannon didn't pull the plugs, these robots would begin killing the governors who were fighting so hard to help the Earth survive its population explosion.

So I had to stop the robots myself.

But I already had a plan for that. Because of the other fire-related thing that had grabbed my attention. I knew exactly what it would do, because it looked just like the ones at the dome. And I knew exactly what it would do to a robot, because once I'd been beneath one at the wrong time.

"Where's the fire?" Ashley shouted.

I pointed at the ceiling. "There!" Aiming my laser, I shouted the mental command, *Kill!*

An almost invisible red flash of light fired from my finger and burned a hole in the ceiling. I kept firing, and almost instantly the ceiling burst into flame.

I knew what to expect, so I had already pulled Ashley toward a table at the side of the hallway.

"Help me lift!" I shouted above the clanging of the fire alarm. We needed to keep our transmission going so the triangulation could finish. "And stand beneath it with me! This is our umbrella!"

The fire in the ceiling triggered the sprinkler system.

Water burst out of the pipes. And as the liquid hit the robot bodies below, they began to topple. The water caused their electric currents to short-circuit. When it had happened to me, back on Mars, I'd awakened with nothing worse than a horrible headache. And that was sure better than brain damage.

Water continued to gush downward, pouring off the table Ashley and I used to protect our robot bodies.

The last of the other robots fell around us.

"It's finished," I said to Ashley. "At least for now."

CHAPTER 23

Cannon snapped his cell phone shut and turned to me. "They've got Stronsky, but no sign of Dr. Jordan."

"Jordan had been communicating with Stronsky by audio," I said. "Even though he left when the countdown was at 15 minutes, if he was in a car he could have been miles away while Stronsky led the robots to the summit."

"Miles away?" Cannon shook his head. "More if he'd left in a helicopter. By the time we got it all cleaned up, he could have made it to a space shuttle and been halfway into orbit. He was like a ghost commander. Untouchable while he sent his army in."

It had only been eight hours since the robot attack in New York City. Already, it seemed to me like it had never happened. I was in my wheelchair, here in the desert mountains of Parker, Arizona, under a clear blue afternoon sky. It was a world away from the noise and pollution of New York City, where the Combat Force was loading the robot bodies into a truck.

"There's going to be a lot to clean up back there," Cannon said, as if he were reading my thoughts. "Including the Terratakers' penetration of the World United Federation. We knew that some soldiers had turned against us, but all those guards . . ."

I heard Cannon's words, but I was only half listening. My attention had turned to the kids now stepping out into the sunlight. Nate and Ashley had been helping them out of the jelly cylinders while I gave my report to Cannon.

The kids were dressed in clothes that Ashley had found in one of the rooms down a hallway in the Institute. They staggered slightly as they followed Ashley toward the helicopter. I understood why they staggered. I remembered the headache I'd had when my own robot was doused with water back on Mars. And they were probably weak, too, since they'd been in the jelly cylinders for six days, unable to use their own muscles.

Some of the smaller kids, though, found the energy to run and giggle as they pointed to the sky. That, too, I understood. They were free. From their jelly cylinder prison and from Jordan's manipulation.

"Tyce," Cannon began, then stopped as his cell phone rang. "Hang on." He answered.

I waved at Ashley.

She waved back. One of the bigger kids tapped her on the shoulder. She nodded at him and pointed at me. They both walked straight toward me as Cannon stepped away to speak on his cell phone.

"Tyce," Ashley said as she and the kid neared me in my wheelchair, "this is Kurt."

Kurt smiled, showing straight rows of strong, white teeth. He was much taller than Ashley. With his blond hair smoothed back, he looked like a young movie star. That made me dislike him even more.

"Hey," he said kindly. "Glad to meet you. Ashley tells me it's true. You *were* born on Mars." He stuck his hand out to shake mine.

I ignored it.

"Tyce?" Ashley frowned. "Don't be like that. Kurt was just trying to protect the other kids. He really couldn't know we were telling the truth when he got them all to unhook our robot computers."

Kurt held his hand out, keeping his smile in place.

"I've got no problem with that," I snapped back. "But ask him about his little deal with Dr. Jordan."

"Deal?" Kurt arranged his face into a puzzled expression.

"Helping out Dr. Jordan so you could be released earlier."

"I doubt it," Kurt said. But his smile now became uncertain.

"I don't."

"Tyce," Ashley said soothingly, "are you sure? You two didn't get off to the best of starts and—" She stopped.

My face felt like it was set in stone as I stared at her. She saw the anger in my eyes. She knew I was telling the truth. I'd tell her all of it later.

"Oh," she said. She took a small step away from Kurt and a step closer to me. She rested her hand on my arm as I continued to speak.

"The triangulation worked," I said. "It located 10 other pods, and the Federation immediately sent jets with soldiers to each location. From what I've learned from Cannon, there has been no resistance. All the kids are being rescued as we speak."

"That's good news," Kurt said, trying to get back into the conversation. "Boy, if it wasn't for you . . ."

He didn't notice that Ashley was looking at him as if he were covered with dead skunk.

"What I'm getting at," I continued, speaking to Ashley, "is that the general has already talked about letting the kids spend a few months with their parents, then sending any of the families who volunteer to Mars. For two reasons. Once all of this makes the news, people on Earth will see them as the soldiers that Dr. Jordan tried to make them. And with all of us able to work our robots on the surface of Mars, we can speed up the settlement project by decades."

"Good, good," Kurt said smoothly. "Count me in."

"Not a chance," I retorted. I turned my head and spoke to Ashley. "The general has already asked me if I'll take a leadership position among all of us who can handle robots. Which I've accepted. And that means my first request is that Kurt does not go to Mars. In fact, when I told the general about Kurt and Dr. Jordan, Cannon said he'd make sure that Kurt never handles another robot as long as he lives."

Finally Kurt's smile faltered. He tried to speak, but Cannon interrupted. "Tyce, Ashley."

I rolled away, and Ashley followed.

"All of the units have reported successful missions," Cannon said. "Out of the 10 pods, 9 were similar to this. Kids in jelly cylinders."

"The tenth?" I asked.

"Empty," Cannon said. He let out a breath. "And they still haven't found Chad. Or Brian. They're somewhere, with that missing pod." He put his hand on Ashley's shoulder. "We're going to do our best to find your parents for you. And the same with Tyce's father. But I may need your help over the next few weeks. Both of you."

"Sir?" I said. All I wanted was to find my father.

"Early indications have given us a hint of where that pod might be." He paused. "Will the two of you go to the Moon?"

SCIENCE AND GOD

You've probably noticed that the question of God's existence comes up in Robot Wars.

It's no accident, of course. I think this is one of the most important questions that we need to decide for ourselves. If God created the universe and there is more to life than what we can see, hear, taste, smell, or touch, that means we have to think of our own lives as more than just the time we spend on Earth.

On the other hand, if this universe was not created and God does not exist, then that might really change how you view your existence and how you live.

Sometimes science is presented in such a way that it suggests there is no God. To make any decision, it helps to know as much about the situation as possible. As you decide for yourself, I'd like to show in the Robot Wars series that many, many people—including famous scientists—don't see science this way.

As you might guess, I've spent a lot of time wondering about science and God, and I've spent a lot of time reading about what scientists have learned and concluded. Because of this, I wrote a nonfiction book called *Who Made The Moon*? and you can find information about it at www.whomadethemoon.com. If you ever read it, you'll see why science does not need to keep anyone away from God.

With that in mind, I've added a little bit more to this book—a couple of essays about the science in journals one and two of Robot Wars, based on what you can find in *Who Made The Moon?*

Sigmund Brouwer
www.whomadethemoon.com

JOURNAL ONE
ARE YOU AN ALIEN?

Q: Are you an alien?

A: That's exactly how Tyce feels. After all, he's spent his
entire life on Mars—weird as it sounds—and has never seen
Earth before. When he arrives on Earth, he's in awe. Just
think of never having seen a yellow sun, white clouds, and
a blue sky before, and then seeing them for the first time.
Then add to that lots of other sights, like dogs, palm trees,
tall grass, a variety of flowers. Sounds, like birds chirping,
trucks on an interstate, and the roar of a male gator. Smells,
like fish frying and the musty dampness of the Everglades.
Surrounded by all these things you'd never experienced, your
mouth would probably drop open too! You'd be overwhelmed.
And who could blame you?

It wouldn't help, either, if somebody made fun of you, even

in a teasing way, like Wild Man did to Tyce. "Where exactly are you from? Mars or something?" Little did Wild Man know how much his teasing bugged Tyce. How it hit home and made Tyce feel even more lonely and afraid. Because he is from another planet. And worse, he's the only true "Martian" on Earth. He's 50 million miles from his home—and everything he knows!

It's no wonder that all of a sudden the dome on Mars looks less scary. Even with all its regulations, like only getting a shower twice a month. Even with all its crises, such as the oxygen leak, a hostile takeover, and almost getting blown up by a black box. Why? Because Earth, as beautiful as it is, will never be Tyce's real home.

Q: Is Earth your true home?

A: All of us have an emptiness that needs to be filled. Some people try to fill it with money or the pursuit of fun. This emptiness truly can make us feel like an alien; some people have described the emptiness as being "homesick for a place you've never been."

Where is that place, the place that lies beyond our life on Earth? Because of his growing faith in God, Tyce has discovered there's more to life than what meets the eye. Than what we can see and touch. He believes that neither Earth nor Mars is his final destination. Instead, someday he'll take an incredible flight to a place called heaven, where he'll live forever with God.

But that doesn't mean we take this beautiful Earth for granted. God wants us to enjoy it. So why not, for the next few days, pretend you're seeing everything on Earth for the first time? Like it's "one giant candy store," as Wild Man said. From plants to insects to reptiles and birds, explore how life swarms this world, cramming each nook and corner. Then you, too, might agree with Nate—that it takes more faith to deny the existence of God than to see a Creator behind all of this.

And then you'll also find it easier to see beyond this Earth to God's ultimate plan for us—to be with him in heaven someday.

JOURNAL TWO
IS IT RIGHT TO MANIPULATE LIFE?

Q: Is it right to manipulate life?

A: That's the very question Tyce Sanders has been asking himself all through this mission. After all, the evil Dr. Jordan is totally controlling the jelly kids' lives, treating them as his slaves. He considers them valuable only because they are part of a very expensive experiment.

Even more, Tyce discovers that Cannon has manipulated his life too. The general is the guy who pushed for the funds that caused Tyce's surgery as a baby. The surgery that went wrong and caused his legs to be useless. Tyce is angry—and he has reason to be.

Is it right to manipulate life?

Although Robot Wars is set in the future, we need to ask ourselves that question now. You don't have to look much farther than the headlines of your newspaper to find out that life is being manipulated today. It all started by genetically manipulating things like corn and beans to give farmers better crops. Then scientists figured out the technology to clone sheep (the first one's name was Dolly), and the genetic material from a jellyfish was successfully implanted into a monkey.

All these things may sound cool, but they could lead to scary places in the future. Like what's happening at the Institute on Earth in A.D. 2040, where defenseless kids are being implanted with spinal plugs so they can control robots.

In short, scientists are rapidly becoming more and more able to manipulate the building blocks of life. But the debates on whether this is right or wrong and how far we should go lag far behind the scientific advances. In other words, we as humans are learning how to do many things before we as a society are able to decide whether we should do them.

Is it right to manipulate life? Is it okay for Dr. Jordan to use the jelly kids as an experiment?

The Terratakers are like those who believe that humans consist of nothing more than complicated arrangements of protein and water. To the Terratakers, then, humans are in control, and they have the right to decide who should live and who should die. Following this philosophy means to people like Dr. Jordan that the "powerful" people can use the "less powerful" people as their slaves. And that the "powerful" people have more value to society than the "less powerful" people, like the jelly kids.

But that's not what Tyce, his parents, Ashley, Nate, and Rawling believe. As Christians, they believe that God created the world. That he created each human being uniquely, and that all human beings are equally valuable in his eyes. And as the one who created us, he and only he should have power over our life and death. Not people like Dr. Jordan, who threaten to use death chips to manipulate others through fear.

When you believe in God, you also have to believe that every life—including your own—is valuable. And that it deserves to be treated with respect.

ABOUT THE AUTHOR

Sigmund Brouwer, his wife, recording artist Cindy Morgan, and their daughters split living between Red Deer, Alberta, Canada, and Nashville, Tennessee. He has written several series of juvenile fiction and eight novels. Sigmund loves sports and plays golf and hockey. He also enjoys visiting schools to talk about books. He welcomes visitors to his Web site at www.coolreading.com.

Tyce's saga continues. . . .

Life in an experimental community on Mars is filled with adventure, new discoveries, and questions. Follow 14-year-old virtual-reality specialist Tyce Sanders as he fights more battles in his quest for truth in Robot Wars.

Read all 5 books in the Robot Wars series

#1 *Death Trap*

#2 *Double Cross*

#3 *Ambush*

#4 *Counterattack*

#5 *Final Battle*

All books available now!

CP0280

The Wormling

From the minds of Jerry B. Jenkins and Chris Fabry comes a thrilling new action-packed fantasy that pits ultimate evil against ultimate good.

Book I
The Book of the King

Book II
The Sword of the Wormling

Book III
The Changeling

Book IV
The Minions of Time

Book V
The Author's Blood

All 5 books available now!

CP0138

Tim Carhardt is drifting through life with one goal—survival. Jamie Maxwell believes she can become—no, *will* become—the first female winner of the cup. But life isn't always as easy as it seems. What happens when dreams and faith hit the wall?

#1 *Blind Spot*
#2 *Over the Wall*
#3 *Overdrive*
#4 *Checkered Flag*

The four-book RPM series spans a year of the chase for the cup. Each story is filled with fast-paced races as well as fast-paced adventure off the track.

All four books available now!